Table of Contents

The
Proxy
Brides
A Bride for
Arthur
CYNDI RAYE

A Bride for Arthur
by
Cyndi Raye
A Proxy Bride Book
Book 27

Book Cover Artist
by
Virginiamckevitt.com[2]

****

1. http://www.CyndiRaye.com

2. http://www.virginiamckevitt.com

Make sure to join the **Proxy Brides Reader's Group**[3]
(https://www.facebook.com/groups/247297295974312/)
to find out when the next book releases!

Thank you to *Rory Lemond* for coming up with the names of the two goats in the story.
Welcome Sparky & Jelly to the Murdock Farm!

---

3. https://www.facebook.com/groups/247297295974312/

Chapter 1

Arthur held the winning cards in his hand. A lock of dark brown hair hung down over his brow, hiding a knowing look of triumph from the three men sitting at the old fashioned round table in the bunkhouse. He took another slug of his drink, laughing to himself because he knew it was plain water and not alcohol like the others had.

The biggest rule on his ranch was no drinking to the point of obliteration. It was the one thing he would not tolerate. He didn't mind if the men had a drink or two after a hard day's work, or even a night in town after a cattle drive, but he didn't tolerate the nonsense that went with drinking.

With a ranch as large as his, Arthur needed all the men to get along. Drinking caused trouble. He knew. His father had been a drunkard. It was a wonder Arthur made it through his childhood, but here he sat, owning the biggest cattle ranch in the Dakota Territory.

The men at this table liked to have a few drinks after work. They knew better than to take it over the limit, but it did loosen them up enough they took too many chances playing cards.

"Lay 'em on the table, Arthur." Edward threw his cards down revealing a terrible hand.

Harry stared at him for a moment, a thick cigar between his teeth. "You think you're going to win again, boss?"

"Stop calling me boss. We've been friends since we were knee-high to a grasshopper, Harry."

The man shrugged. "You're still my boss, boss!" He laughed at his own joke, then immediately pulled the cigar out of his mouth and began to cough when he sucked in a cloud of smoke. He threw the hand down he was holding, face up.

"Walt, your turn," Arthur prompted. He was bored with the game, but he didn't want to go to the house yet. Sometimes it was too quiet there.

His foreman grunted. Walt was older than they were, with gray hair peppered over a set of thick black hair. He mostly wore a wide-brimmed hat to hide his age and had the ladies crawling all over him when he went to town. Walt liked the attention. He stared at Arthur for a minute, trying to read his face. Then, like always, he set his hand down, thinking it was going to be the winning one.

Arthur laid his own hand down, smiling. Especially when the moans and groans followed. He reached for the pot and slid the winnings across the table.

"Don't you have enough money, boss?"

Arthur grinned. "There's never enough. Wanna play another round?" Although his limbs ached from chopping wood today, he wasn't ready to turn in yet, or sit in that big house alone. Lately it really bothered him. He couldn't say why.

Three men shook their heads.

"I promised Ida that I'd take her for a walk this evening. We're going to watch the sun set." Harry tugged on his cigar.

Arthur's brow rose. "I tried that once, but a simple walk always turns a woman into thinking I'm wanting to dish out a marriage proposal."

"You haven't walked or talked with a woman in a long time. Don't you think it's time you do?" Harry lifted his chin and blew smoke in the air.

The other men nodded. Walt tapped his calloused hands on the table. "Arthur, it's time you think about your legacy. Who are you going to pass on this enormous ranch to if there is no family?"

Walt had been badgering him about that a lot lately. Arthur had worked hard to build up the biggest and wealthiest ranch and he did it, despite all the blocks in the road. But, he had no one to share it with. "It seems every woman in the past two years wants me for one reason. They want the ranch and all it offers. I've seen that happen before. It can drive a man to drink."

Like his father.

"You can't let what happened to your father ruin your chances of happiness. His life was his own to destroy. This ranch was handed to him by your grandfather and he pissed it all away. Then you came along and built it back up, even better than your grandfather ever did. It's now the biggest ranch in the area. Why wouldn't you want to share that with someone?"

Arthur didn't know why. All he knew was his father had loved his mother so much that when she died, he began to drink. Everything he had lived for didn't matter any longer. Not even the fact he had a son to raise. When he got older, Arthur understood his father's lack of caring had been because of his great loss, but not dealing with it put him in an early grave.

Arthur wanted someone to love him for himself, not because they had to or because he had money. "I don't want a woman who loves my money more than me."

Walt nodded in understanding, but he wasn't letting Arthur off the hook. "You come here almost every night to play a game of cards because you don't want to spend the night in that big, lonely house. It would be nice to see a family there, kids running around, a wife that you can tolerate. Don't you think, men?"

Edward and Harry nodded. "It's time you do something about that, boss," Harry told him. "I've known you a long time. You worked hard for years. It's time to find yourself a decent woman and settle down."

Arthur frowned. "What about you, Harry? You're a darn good ranch hand and my best friend. Why don't you do the same?"

"I've got my eye on Ida. Who knows what will happen in the next few months." The smile on his best friend's face told Arthur all he needed to know. If Harry asked for Ida's hand in marriage, Arthur would offer them one of the cabins on the property.

This ranch was expansive, and he'd find a home for each of his men if they needed it. After all, they had all stuck with him over the scrawny years when he was struggling to turn the ranch into something big. It turned out the ranch became bigger than his grandfather had ever even imagined. Giving back to his men would be Arthur's way of paying them for their dedication to him and the Bar M Ranch. "If it gets serious, you know you always have a home here."

"Thanks, Arthur. Now, let's get back to your dilemma."

"I don't have a dilemma."

The three men smirked. Arthur looked around. They were up to something.

Harry pulled something out of his pocket. He unfolded a piece of torn newspaper and handed it to Arthur. "Take a look at this."

Arthur took the paper and began to read. "Wanted: Do you live in the remote west and find yourself in need of a bride? Marriage by Proxy will guarantee a bride of your choosing."

He threw the paper on the table. "What is this, like a mail order bride? You know that doesn't work? I know a dozen men who sent money for train tickets and the ladies never showed up. Why, it happened to Arnold Fox just last week."

Harry tapped his finger on the newspaper. "That's why you need to marry a bride by proxy, boss. You can pick the bride and the ceremony has to happen on each end before they leave home. Plus, you can add a clause in the contract and if she doesn't suit, get it annulled within a period of time. I was reading up on it before I met Ida."

"It does sound like a sensible idea, especially since she won't know how wealthy I truly am. Not like the ladies from around here do. But, the fact remains that when she gets here, will she care about me or my money, so it won't work."

Edward had been quiet for most of the conversation. "It can work if she doesn't know how wealthy you are. When you mentioned that Harry can have one of the cabins on the property if he gets hitched to Ida, why not do the same thing for yourself?"

Arthur was getting a bad taste in his mouth. "You've got to be kidding?"

"Nope, not kidding. Remember when you bought those two hundred acres from old man Wilson's boy after he passed on? The one that is attached to your property? The house and barn are still sitting there, abandoned."

Arthur hadn't thought about the old Wilson farm. He really didn't know what to do with it and forgot it even existed until now.

Walt piped in. "That's a great idea. We need to up the stakes a bit. Arthur needs to make his proxy bride fall in love with him and not his money within two months from the time she gets here. He can't mention that he owns the Bar M Ranch. She has to believe he owns the dilapidated Wilson farm."

Harry shook his head and held up a hand. "There has to be a big enough wager so he goes through with this."

"What about Henry and Lami?"

Arthur's eyes widened. "There's no amount of money you can give me for my two horses."

The men laughed when Walt spoke up. "That's why we want you to agree to this. If you lose and she asks for an annulment before the two months are up, you have to hand over your two prized horses to us."

"No deal. I'm not wagering my horses."

Edward shook his head. "He thinks he's King Arthur and the two horses are descendants from those days. Henry is short for Hengroen and Lami is short for Llamrai, the same names King Arthur gave to his two favorites."

Arthur gave Edward a hard look. "So what?"

Edward leaned in. "I knew you didn't have the guts to try."

"You are trying to strong arm me into taking the wager."

"Yes, I am. You need it, Arthur. If you don't try, you will live in that house alone forever, or maybe you won't but it will be with someone who you'll never know if they love you for yourself or for your money. You said so yourself."

His words brought Arthur up short. "I know you mean well, but, my horses? Anything but Henry and Lami."

Arthur looked around the table to find three men adamantly shaking their heads.

"We won't be here forever, Arthur. If I marry Ida, I'll be getting all cozy every night in my own home. Edward's been thinking of getting himself a proxy bride some day and Walt, he'll soon be old and hard of hearing. Who are you going to keep company with?"

They were right. He didn't want to admit it, but without his men every evening, he'd be sitting on his porch alone. "I don't want to wager my horses."

"It's the only thing that will make you try, Arthur. Besides, we aren't going to make it easy for you."

Arthur gritted his teeth. "Well, then, men, bring it on. You know me, I love a challenge."

Chapter 2

Gwen shivered. Not from the cold since it was a warm, autumn day. But the winter was coming and the air would be so raw outside, it would freeze her if she didn't find a solution to her current situation. She hurried past the rows of brick homes and buildings until she came to her own. Turning the knob, she lifted her skirts and ran up the three flights of stairs, out of breath by the time she entered the small apartment she shared with her two co-workers.

Hanging her light shawl on the hook inside the door, she scrubbed her hands and poured a cup of tea. Joining the other two, who were not their normal happy selves, she gave them both a look of encouragement. "What shall we do now, ladies?"

Alice hung her head. Gwen was sure there were tears in her eyes. "We're done for. You know what we have to do if we can't find work? Let's face it, Gwen, who is going to give us a job this time of year?"

Gwen had to agree with Alice, but it didn't mean they had to give up. "I know it's tough out there, but we have to find a solution for all of us. In exactly twenty-eight days, we will be homeless when our lease runs out."

Bessie shook her head and stared at Gwen, the sparkle gone from the woman's blue eyes. "I don't see how you can be so positive.

This whole situation is terrible. We've worked at the factory for three years. The long hours have taken a toll on us, but at least we had a job. Now, we have nothing."

Gwen piped in. "You have to look at it from a new perspective. This is a new opportunity. Why, every single day you mention how you want to be a nurse. Why not apply at The Belleview Hospital School of Nursing? Besides, your aunt told you she'd help."

"Where do I live while I go to school? We are losing the only home I was happy in."

"Oh, Bessie. I know you hated to live at your aunt's house before we got this place, but at least take a look at the opportunity. They may house you while you learn how to become a nurse. Why don't you try? We still have almost a month left on our lease here."

Bessie sniffed and then nodded. There was nothing like having to make a decision when your back was against the wall. As far as Gwen was concerned, at least Bessie had her aunt. They may not get along and agree with each other, but her aunt had always told her if things didn't work out living on her own, she'd allow Bessie to come back.

Alice was always the quiet one. She had been staring into her cup of tea, not saying much. But when she looked up at Gwen there was a sparkle in her eye and a glint of recklessness in her glance.

Gwen gave her a look. "What are you up to, Miss Alice? I suppose you already have something up your sleeve?"

"I do." She pulled a page from a newspaper out of her pocket and handed it to Gwen.

"What is this?"

"Read it."

Gwen did. "Proxy Brides needed!" She scanned the article and noticed the address of the agency was right down the street around the corner. "Isn't that the same place they have the matchmaker agency?"

Alice nodded. "Yes, dear, it is. It seems the mail order bride industry is slowing somewhat. Men are sending money for train tickets and the brides are not showing up. So, these same men want a guarantee the women they pick will make the trip. Hence, a proxy bride."

"Are you thinking of becoming a bride by proxy?" The thought hadn't occurred to Gwen before.

"Yes. I think we both should try."

"You do?"

"You can't go back home, Gwen. Not to a father who drinks like he does and a stepmother who hates you. You hated it there."

Gwen knew she would never return home. Her father had been on the verge of becoming violent. He had raised a hand to her several times and stopped himself. She was well aware it would only be a matter of time before he hit her. His drinking was getting worse. She hadn't seen or heard from him these past three years she'd been on her own but she heard rumors he was out of control.

"I know I did," Gwen told her. "I did try to visit several times, but he wouldn't see me. He hates that I left. You know I gave up visiting after those few times."

"It's for the best. Now, on to the future. Let's do this. We may find a wonderful man that will give us a lovely home. Not only will he be promised a wife, but at least we know we'll be married before we even go."

"How are we going to be sure he is a good man? I don't want someone like my father."

"Let's go visit this agency right now."

Bessie began to sniffle again. "I'll walk along until we get to my aunt's house so I can speak with her."

"Of course, dear," Alice told her. "Now, ladies, let's get on with our future!"

*****

A week and a half later, Alice and Gwen were sitting in the matchmaker's office for the second time, staring at the middle-aged woman across from them. "Good morning, ladies, and welcome back. I have the best news. There has been a match for the both of you. Who wants to go first?"

Gwen spoke up. "Since this was Alice's idea, I think she should be the first."

The woman nodded. Her dark hair was pulled away from her face, secured in a tight bun. She wore a crisp white blouse with a darker skirt and stood while she spoke. "Very well. Alice, Randall Kepple from Colorado City needs a proxy bride right away. He comes from a well known family there and has an established hotel that has been promised to him by his late grandfather. There were stipulations. If he marries by the end of the month, the hotel will be solely his. Otherwise, he must share with his two step-sisters who plan to sell the hotel. The marriage by proxy suits him better than waiting on a mail order bride, especially since he doesn't have time to make sure she shows up. Can you be there by the end of the month?"

Alice jumped up and gave the woman a hug. "I can be there by the end of the week!"

"That's even better. Prepare for a proxy marriage today. I'll make the arrangements while you go home to pack."

"Isn't that way too fast?" Gwen also stood up, wondering how they can make this happen so quickly.

"It is all arranged ahead of time. Besides, I will get a bonus if I can pull this off sooner than later."

Gwen was concerned about the woman receiving a bonus. Did she have their best interest at heart? "I don't dispute the way you do things here, but how can we know the man isn't some horrible person and will treat her badly?"

"Sit down, Gwen." The matchmaker sat across from her, before rifling through a neat stack of papers on her desk. "Here is the application the groom has to fill out before we accept him to our agency."

She stayed silent while Gwen read the extensive application. "Well, men don't always tell the truth."

Miss Wanda gave her a reassuring smile. "No they do not. That is why an investigator from our agency is sent to make sure the man is suitable. We do not compromise a woman's integrity or safety. That is why we are paid so much, along with a bonus to find decent women for them if they are in a hurry."

Gwen felt better knowing they were protected in that way. "Thank you for explaining."

"You are welcome. Now, are you ready to hear about Mr. Murdock?"

Gwen gave her a solemn nod. She was anxious now. If the man was investigated, he had to be decent, didn't he?

"Mr. Arthur Murdock is a farmer with a two hundred acre spread near Green River, Dakota Territory. It is remote and he is looking for a bride who doesn't mind not getting into town often. He also added a clause to the proxy contract stipulating that either of you can annul the marriage after a two month grace period. He understands the hardships of living on a ranch out in the wilderness but would like his proxy bride to give it at least two months."

Gwen had to think a bit. "It doesn't sound as if he has much faith the marriage will work?"

"He needs someone to give him encouragement. Through our interview process, we found out his father was a heavy drinker and his life didn't end well. Arthur was belittled and doesn't think too much of himself. He needs a bride to show him kindness. Can you do that, Gwen?"

"Yes, I understand far too well the consequences of a parent that imbibes."

Miss Wanda nodded. "I know, it was why I chose you for this proxy marriage instead of your friend. Is that a yes?"

Gwen nodded. "Why not? There is absolutely nothing here for me."

"Good. Since Alice's ceremony will be today, why don't we set yours up for tomorrow morning? I will secure a ticket for you to be on your way and make all the arrangements."

"I really didn't think it would happen so quickly."

"That's the wonder of a matchmaking service. One just never knows what cupid has in store."

"I don't plan to fall in love. All I want is a secure, decent life."

Miss Wanda gave her a knowing smile. "Everyone tells me that. I've got tons of letters from women who tell me differently. Now, be on your way so I can finish here. Good day, Gwen. You won't regret your decision."

Chapter 3

Town of Bryan on the Black Forks of the Green River
Dakota Territory

The locomotive shook and shivered as it came to a dead stop. Gwen had been holding her breath, tired and dusty from the intense ride over mountainous tracks and gorges. It was beautiful here, how the land swept along rolling hills and mountains so high in the distance she had to press her face against the window to see it all.

The town of Bryan was as close as she was going to get to her destination. Green River didn't have a railroad yet, but one of the conductors announced by this time next year it would.

In the meantime, she'd have to travel the rest of the way to Green River by stage. A few of the passengers moaned when they heard the railroad had chosen Bryan to lay tracks to instead of Green River and had to go by coach the rest of the way. She had never been on a stage so she didn't know if it was going to be enjoyable at all. It had to be better than this rattletrap train ride.

One of the passengers looked at her, shaking his head. "We'll be traveling another full day to get to our destination. I hate stage coaches. They are gruelling and hard on the body."

Gwen turned her head, pretending she hadn't heard. She wasn't looking forward to another full day of riding in a contraption that was uncomfortable.

The conductor announced they could get off now. She steadied herself as she departed, holding a small carpet bag in one hand and grabbing the cold rail as she took herself down the steel steps. Gwen checked at the window to make sure the stage was going to be here soon since she didn't see anyone waiting at the depot. Digging through her reticule to pay for another ticket, a deep voice called out.

"Are you Mrs. Gwen Murdock?"

Her head snapped towards the voice. She had one hand in her purse and her mouth fell open when she saw the tall cowboy standing a foot away. He was indeed one of the most handsome men she'd ever come in contact with. "I'm Mrs. Murdock." The sound of her married name came out in a low whisper. It was so odd to say the name.

He held out a hand. "I'm Arthur Murdock."

She stared at his outstretched hand for a moment before placing her own in his. It was warm and she felt the callouses on his fingers, surprising her at first. Of course his hands would be rough. He wrapped those fingers around her own in a friendly shake.

"How do you do?" When she gazed into his eyes, she was startled at first. They were friendly and warm, not cold and bloodshot like her father's had been. Here was a man who had his wits about him. Worried she had married someone like her own father had her inhaling deeply. She let out the air slowly and gave him a smile of relief.

"We best get moving. We'll be on the road for a long time. My buggy is right over yonder." He pointed to a small horse and wagon a few feet away.

Once she was settled on the wooden seat next to him, she gave him a brief smile. "Thank you for coming to pick me up. I was expecting to ride the stage to Green River."

He shook his head. "No sense in doing that when the farm is halfway between here and Green River."

"Farm? I thought you had a ranch?"

He gave her a long stare. "Two hundred acres is a farm to me. I guess you can call it a ranch if you want to."

He seemed offended but she wasn't sure why. "I can call it whatever you like. It is your home."

"It's yours now, too," he mumbled, staring straight ahead. She was able to peruse him from where she sat. He seemed manly, with a strong profile and jawline. He wore a wide brimmed hat but it looked like he had dark hair underneath the hat from the strands that stuck out at his neck. His buttoned down shirt was rolled up at the sleeves. Strong, muscular hands held the rawhide straps that guided the horse.

She decided that the matchmaker had chosen a very virile and handsome husband for her. It made her smile. Of course, he picked that moment to turn his head. "What are you all giddy about?"

She shrugged. "This new adventure. It's beautiful here, nothing like the city."

"You may as well relax. It's going to be hours until we arrive."

Gwen must've dozed at one point. She awoke with a start when the wagon came to a stop. How had she fallen asleep so quickly? They were off the road, under a tall tree with leaves so thick it kept them dry from the rain that was coming down like a water fall.

"We'll sit here for a few minutes until the rain stops."

"I'm sorry. I didn't mean to fall asleep."

"Train rides can be tiring. I'm sure you didn't rest much in the last few days bouncing around on that contraption."

"I'm afraid you are right. It is quite annoying."

They were making small talk. It was strange sitting beside this man who was her husband now. Did they need to discuss the arrangement? Maybe she should bring it up. "I'm wondering if we need to talk about our proxy marriage?"

He turned and looked into her eyes. When he did, it startled her. There was great confusion in her head. Why was he looking at her as if she was a mouse and he were the cat ready to pounce? It totally confused her. Emotions she hadn't known existed sprung up, causing her even more anxiety.

He grinned then, which gave her some relief. "I guess we should. We will have sixty days to see if we like each other. I'm guessing you wanted to marry a man like me with a productive farm or you wouldn't be here."

She smiled. "My situation wasn't ideal. I've lived in the city all my life. It may take me some time to get used to living in the country."

He nodded. "Are you running from something? Or, someone?"

"No, of course not. I'm going to be honest with you and I hope you do the same. My job ended. The factory I worked in shut its doors, leaving me without work. I leased an apartment with two friends who also worked there. At the end of the month the lease ran out and we had no job or money to go anywhere else. This seemed like the only solution."

"I see. You have no plans to fall in love then? Just looking for a roof over your head?"

He made it sound so cold. But, it was the truth. "It does sound like I'm a gold digger, doesn't it?"

He gave her a huge smile and shook his head. "Not at all. I'd probably do what's best for me if I were in your situation. Besides, when you see the farm you'll realize the truth in the matter. There's no gold in my farm. Just a man working to make a living."

She shrugged, starting to like the man. He seemed honest and didn't make excuses for what he had. "It's the only life I've known. Working in a hot factory day after day for long hours was not easy. At least you have fresh air out here and a sky that looks so blue it amazes me."

He followed her gaze and looked up. "That we do when it's not raining. Right now it's a pale gray."

She didn't think either one of them realized the storm had passed. The sky, even though it was gray from the rain, began to clear up. White clouds began to roll around the skies once again and she noticed how blue it turned so quickly.

"You hungry?" he asked.

"A little."

He reached into the back of the wagon to pull out a basket. Opening it up, he handed her some fresh bread and a block of cheese. "My cook packed a few things."

She stared at him. "You have a cook?"

His cheek twitched for a moment. "I mean the ranch next to my property. I also work there at times, helping to train the horses. It's extra money, which you'll find we can always use over the winter months when things are tough here. I've grown quite close to their cook, who treats me like a son. When she heard I was coming to get you, Ida sent this along."

"How nice of her. I hope to meet her sometime."

"I'm not sure she will come to the farm." He spoke rather quickly. "She's old and feeble. I don't think she likes to leave the ranch often. She has a bad limp and uses a cane. It's hard for her to get around."

Gwen bit into the fresh bread. "Mm, well, she knows how to bake."

"That she does." He sunk his teeth in also. Gwen had the feeling he took a bite so he didn't have to explain anything more about the cook.

Ten minutes later they were on their way, riding along rolling hills that sparkled and gleamed in the crisp air. The rain shower had everything all wet, but the sun that was now out slowly began to dry out the land. She was content to sit on the wooden bench and enjoy the scenery.

Right as they came out of a bend in the road, a huge sign stood out. The letters were clean and large. Bar M Ranch, it read.

Arthur pointed. "That's our neighbor who I work for now and again. Sometimes he'll get a horse in that is hard to train and hire me to get the job done."

"You must be good with horses."

He nodded. "I am. I'm not a braggart, but I've grown up here, where they run free. I've had my share of wild ones over the years. It takes patience. The owner of the Bar M doesn't have that."

She shook her head. "That's too bad. You'd think if you own a big ranch, patience would be a priority."

"Not for him. I'd rather not associate with him except when the horses need a skilled hand. It helps pay the bills."

"I hope I don't have to talk with him then. He sounds hideous."

That made Arthur smile. "Oh, he is hideous and hard to look at. I'd best stay away if I were you. Don't go on that land at all. He's not nice if you haven't asked permission to be there." He kept his eyes straight ahead as he spoke.

The land seemed to go on and on forever. "Is this still Bar M land?"

He nodded. "It will go on for some time before we go down our lane."

She liked how he said our lane, as if he were including her already. Without even knowing her, she was again finding him to be quite kind. She placed a hand on his sleeve. "Thank you for making this transition easy for me."

He gave her a smile. A dimple in his left cheek had her staring at him. When she looked up, she saw the amused look in his eyes. She turned away.

Thirty minutes later he pointed. "This is it. We'll turn down here."

They rode for another ten minutes down a bumpy lane, but the horse didn't seem to mind at all. The strong mare side-stepped a few rocks in its path and kept going. There were a few times when Gwen had to hang onto Arthur's arm to keep herself from being thrown off the bench. She looked back at the rolling hills wondering if it was part of their land. "Is that property part of the farm?"

He shook his head. "That belongs to the Bar M Ranch. I've got a little spread that butts up against it. Don't worry, you will love it even if it isn't quite as fancy as the Bar M."

Gwen wasn't sure what to expect. The road was grown over with weeds, along with big ruts and rocks in the way. "Doesn't anyone clear the road here?"

"Not much. It takes too much time away from my other work. You know, the important stuff that keeps food on the table. Do you know how to take care of a garden?"

"I can learn." She didn't know what else to say. Living in the city and working long hours at a factory didn't give her much time to grow anything. She was too tired after a ten to twelve hour day to even try to grow a flower in the window.

"We'll till the ground for next year's planting. The ground will be ready for next spring."

Gwen didn't understand. "Why not wait until next spring?"

Arthur gave her a passing glance. "It's the way we do things here. I don't know why."

Gwen wondered about that too. He didn't quite answer any of her questions right. She knew when a person was sidestepping the issue.

Gwen had a funny feeling Arthur was doing just that and she wasn't sure if she should be worried or not. Time would tell.

Chapter 4

Arthur was trying hard to answer every question as diligently as possible, but she was quite inquisitive. Her beauty was almost blinding and he wondered how she got out of the big city without a man asking for her hand.

While she watched the rolling hills, he had turned to stare. Her skin was so pale, he'd have to make sure she wore a hat outside to keep it from burning. She had dark hair that she pulled back showing her beautiful high cheeks and long, dark eyes. When she had looked at him before, her eyes were inquisitive, staring at him as if he had the answer to the world's problems. It was unnerving to say the least.

She may not be too happy that he agreed to a dumb fool's game from bored men who had nothing better to do. Arthur was already starting to regret involving such a beautiful woman. He should probably stop right now and tell her the truth.

Then he spotted his two horses along the fence line. Harry and Edward had them saddled and were riding them hard and fast right in his line of vision. They were deliberately teasing, to remind him why he was in this current situation.

Gwen pointed and drew in her breath. "Would you take a look at those horses? They are gorgeous! I've never seen such beauty before."

He was proud of the two horses he had grown to love more than any of the others he had trained. "That's Henry and Lami. They are quite exquisite. Henry is a stallion and Lami is a mare. They are partners for life."

She turned to him, her eyes lit up. "Are they yours?"

He wanted to say yes, they were his prized possessions but knew if he failed this wager, he'd lose them. The rules were simple. If he told her about the wager in the sixty days they were at the farm, he'd have to hand over the horses. Arthur scrubbed his eyes with the back of his hand. He had to remind himself he was a pauper with an old farm they'd have to make the best of. "I'm afraid they belong to the owner of the Bar M Ranch." That wasn't a lie.

The two riders slowed and turned towards them, waving their hands in the air. "Howdy neighbors! We'll be by sometime soon to get acquainted."

Arthur raised his hand in the air. He didn't comment either way. Gwen gave them a big smile and waved both her hands back and forth. "Howdy, neighbors." Then she giggled and turned to him. "They seem friendly enough."

Arthur wasn't looking forward to watching her face fall when she saw the place they were going to live in for the next sixty days. As they continued on down the bumpy trail, they came around a corner and in the opening stood an old one story house with a huge barn. The yard was overgrown with weeds. Certain trees had been starting to loose some of their leaves while the pine trees stood big and tall along the edge of the yard.

Arthur slowly turned towards Gwen. She was staring at the house, her eyes huge. The look on her face wasn't disgust or frightful, but of amazement. Then she whispered, "Is this your home?"

He didn't say a word but watched as she got down from the buggy and turned around in the yard like a small child in her glory, taking everything in. Her arms were outstretched and she flung her head back and looked up at the white clouds.

Arthur was amazed and enamored of this woman who took in an old dilapidated house and barn as if it were a mansion. Maybe her eyesight was bad. "It needs some repair," he told her, hopping down from the buggy.

She nodded. "It sure does and we'll work hard to give the house life again. I can't wait to get started!"

Her enthusiasm surprised him. When Arthur turned to take another long look at the house, he tried to see it through her eyes. She was from New York City, where everything was so close together, the houses built side by side for city blocks at a time. He had been there once. There were no rolling hills or even much grass in the city. She probably wasn't used to seeing so much land.

"Would you like to take a look inside?"

She glanced at the buggy. "I can go ahead of you if you'd like to take care of the horse first."

She was smart, too. He was trying to make her comfortable and her concern was for the horse. He was going to like her already. "I'll bring your carpetbag along when I come in."

Arthur watched her glide across the yard, her hips swaying gently as she pulled the hem of her skirt up from hitting the high weeds. Even the high weeds didn't seem to bother her one bit. He was pleasantly surprised that she hadn't run the other way.

He took care of the mare and put her to pasture. She was brought down from the ranch yesterday. She'd be alone here for the next sixty days without the company of the rest of the horses. He'd have to give her special attention. He leaned in and whispered to her. She perked up as if listening to him. "You'll have plenty of space all by yourself, Ellie. I'll make sure to bring you some extra apples and carrots." Her ears twitched and she stared at him, big brown eyes waiting.

Arthur pulled a carrot from his pocket and she tugged at it until she had it in her mouth. Ellie walked off, nibbling on the carrot as if it was expected of her to receive a treat for taking them to town. He shook his head, closing the gate to the corral.

Arthur's men had come here for the last few days making slight repairs. The place had fallen apart since the old man got sick. Arthur felt ashamed for not checking in on the old man to see if he needed any help. He had assumed the three sons were helping here, but found out later they left him to die alone. When he offered to buy the property the three sons had argued price until Arthur had made them an offer and told them to take it or leave it. No one else would buy the property in the shape it was in.

He knew their greed would show through and it did. They accepted his offer and the place had been sitting empty ever since. Arthur hadn't thought about it much after the sale since he didn't know what to do with it. At least now it had come in handy.

Making his way casually across the yard towards the house, Arthur was carrying Gwen's heavy carpetbag in one hand and lifted his hat from his head with his other. He wasn't in a hurry, figuring he'd give her time to peruse the house.

That is until he heard a blood-curling scream coming from inside as he stood at the front door.

*****

Gwen had been excited to take a look at the inside of the house. At least the porch was sturdy. She went up the three wide wooden steps noticing they had been repaired. Some of the planks had been replaced with new, fresh wood. At least he cared enough to make the repairs.

The front door was slightly ajar. Frowning, she pushed it open to find a huge room inside. Looking around, she wondered how in the world a man lived in such filth. Dust bunnies covered the corners while cobwebs ran from wall to wall. What did he do, duck underneath them? It made no sense.

She walked around the large room, realizing her new husband was a slob. She shook her head right before she gave herself a shake. This was still better than living on the streets or back with her father and step-mother. At least she'd be able to sweep the dirt outside.

Placing hands on her hips she noticed a huge fireplace along the far wall in the parlor, two chairs and a long settee. A large window looked out over the front yard. She peeked out to see Arthur coming across the overgrown lawn. He looked like a man who worked hard, she just wasn't sure exactly what he did. It sure didn't look like he did anything here.

Gwen turned to take a look at the rest of the small house. It was perfect for the two of them. She went through a small archway to find a kitchen with small cook-stove, along with a huge table to work on and several shelves loaded with dishes and pans. Cobwebs covered the dishes. How in the world did he cook?

Then she saw the pot sitting on the small cook-stove. She walked over to touch the pot. It was still warm. Lifting the lid, the smell of chicken stew wafted through her nostrils. Since he had been on the road to pick her up she knew he had not done the cooking. Perhaps it was the old woman Ida that he spoke of. She made a mental note to thank her when she had the chance.

A small plate covered with a towel revealed fresh bread. Gwen's belly rumbled. It had been a long day. She was tired and was so happy she didn't have to do any cooking tonight.

There was a door on the far wall. Figuring it was the bedroom, she walked across the floor and stopped right in front of the closed door. There were noises coming from the closed room. She tried to place an ear against the door, but then she jumped back when her weight pushed it open.

She stepped inside to find two black and white goats standing in the middle of the room. One had small horns protruding from his head while the other began to make a horrible loud noise. They turned to her, startled, stiffened their legs like a rod and fell over.

She screamed! It came out so hard and fast it surprised even Gwen. She had never been so scared in all of her life. Now look what she had done!

"What is it?" Arthur was behind her, carrying her carpetbag in one hand and holding his hat in the other. He let the carpetbag fall to the floor and came over to her.

She pointed to the goats on the floor. "I've killed them."

Arthur frowned. He looked at the goats lying on the floor, their legs stiff as a wooden post. "They are not dead."

"What? I saw them roll their eyes at me and fall to the ground."

He began to walk through the door. She decided to follow him since he was in the lead. She tip-toed behind him, not even knowing why. What she should do is get out of here now. Instead, when he stopped she butted up against him.

That was more shocking than watching the goats die. His warm body gave her pause. She quickly stepped back, more confused than ever. Her emotions were all over the place and she didn't know whether to laugh or cry.

"See, I told you."

The two goats that had been lying sideways on the ground now shook themselves off and got up. The one with the horns began to walk towards Gwen. "What is it doing?" she asked, horrified. What in tarnation had happened? "How did they rise from the dead?"

Arthur laughed. "I get that reaction a lot. These are special goats. The ranch owner next door bought them in Tennessee from an old friend who brought a small herd from Nova Scotia two years ago. They have some type of genetic disorder that makes their legs paralysed and they faint when they get startled."

"Why do you have them in your house if they are your neighbors?"

"When I work at the ranch they follow me home. So the rancher next door said to let them stay and sooner or later they will find their way back."

"And have they?"

"Have they what?" He asked.

The way Arthur was staring at her with his dark eyes confused her. What was wrong with her? Did she look unkempt? "Have they found their way back? Because I see them in your bedroom and it doesn't look like they are going anywhere soon."

"No, they seem to like it here. I'll put your bag in here and we can clean up and eat some of the stew Ida sent down." With that, he shooed the two goats out the door and closed it in case they tried to get back in.

She'd have to keep an eye on those two goats.

Chapter 5

After they had eaten the stew and fresh bread, she had tried to clean up but Arthur had insisted it wait until morning. He was kind yet firm with her. She had wanted to at least clear the dishes but he had sent her to bed.

She had gotten in her nightgown and crawled under the covers, pulling them up over her chin while waiting for him to arrive. Since she had never even experienced a kiss from a man, she wasn't sure what to expect. It made her nervous thinking about sleeping in the same bed as a man, especially one as handsome as Arthur. As she waited and wondered where he was at, her eyelids grew heavier until she fell asleep.

He never did come into the room. She woke up at the crack of dawn, stretching and looking around the bedroom but he was not there. There was no sign he had ever entered through the closed door. A bit of relief went through Gwen. If he was being a gentleman and giving her time to get to know him, she was very pleased. It made her realize how lucky she was to find a kind man as a proxy husband.

Getting dressed quickly, she made her way to the kitchen to find a plate of warm eggs and more bread on the table where she had sat the night before. A small towel covered the plate to keep it warm. A smile crossed her face as she made her way outside to fill a bowl with water.

Gwen loved her tea. She had brought some along, just in case her husband didn't drink tea. She hurried back inside and poured the water into a small kettle, swished the water around and dumped it in the small basin. Then she poured more water in and set the pot on the stove to heat up. A small fire was still lit in the cook stove. It was nice to get up to a warm house.

In New York, the old furnace in their apartment had made so much noise and the radiators rattled and hissed all night long. The landlord always waited until it was so cold to light the coal furnace and there was always the issue to keep it going. There were times when they woke up in the middle of the night freezing. They'd have to get ready for work in a cold room with frost on the inside of the window panes. By the time they got to work at the factory, they'd spend all day in an overheated factory, with sweat pouring from every crevice of their bodies.

It went on like that all winter long. The three girls had promised each other last winter it would be the last one they'd spend in that cold, drab apartment. She smiled and looked around. They didn't have to find a better place to live now. Each of them had been sent on their own journey.

Gwen sighed. It was nice here. A bit too quiet, even though she had always wanted to hear the sounds of the countryside. Well, now she was really in the country. More than she ever realized. Was she made for this kind of living? She had always lived in the city. It would be a challenge to get used to something else, but she was ready and willing.

She gazed out the window to see Arthur at the barn with a pitch fork in his hand. He was picking up bales of hay from a stack piled there and taking them inside one by one. She smiled, watching him for a few minutes while her tea brewed.

He was a fine looking man, built strong as an ox. The thought made her laugh. If her friends knew she was thinking about his physique so much, they'd be teasing her by now. She gave a sad smile. Would she ever see her two best friends again? At least she had Bessie's aunt's address to write to her. They had all promised to stay in touch.

After finishing her eggs and bread, Gwen decided to start on the kitchen. It was time to put some order into the house. She searched for an apron but didn't see any. Then she gazed out the small window in the backside of the kitchen to see a few items blowing on the wash line outside.

The back door squeaked when she opened it, giving her the impression it wasn't used much, if at all. She hurried across the yard to find the apron and a few towels and rags hanging from the line, stiff as a rock. She thought that was awfully strange to find laundry looking like this after it was laundered.

Gwen decided to take them all down and use the rags and towels for cleaning. Once she dunked them in hot soapy water, they'd be fine. The apron would have to be washed again.

She spent the morning becoming familiar with her kitchen. Gwen treated her new role as a new job and she was very thorough with everything related to work. She took a broom over the ceilings in the kitchen, parlor and bedroom until every single cobweb was a thing of the past.

Satisfied, she filled a bowl with hot, soapy water and washed down the furniture in the living room. Then, after exchanging the dirty water for clean, she took more soapy water to the window in the front of the house and the smaller ones in the kitchen and bedroom. When she had them sparkling, it was much easier to see outside.

Next she tackled the kitchen shelves. Setting every single item on the long table, she washed the shelves first, then washed the dishes, pots and pans next. Letting them all air dry on the long table, she then put them back in an order that made sense to her. Since she'd be the one doing most of the cooking, it was only right she organize the kitchen this way.

Gwen wondered if Arthur was the kind of man who'd care much how she arranged the inside of the house. He seemed awfully busy out in the barn, so she assumed he'd be fine with the work she was doing. If not, he'd have to let her know. They'd have to have a discussion on his inability to keep house. The man was very messy!

She actually took a moment to look around at the work she'd done today. Without taking a break, she had the whole house almost cleaned. It had been a long morning. She was grateful there was no upstairs to worry about.

Gwen did wonder if they had a spring house. She'd have to take a walk outside to find out. They were called that because a small spring ran through to keep the food and milk at a cool temperature. Most farmers built the small stone or wood house around the cool waters. When they had pulled up with the buggy she hadn't bothered to look at what all was here. She just knew from reading a book on pioneer women at the local library that spring houses were necessary to keep food from spoiling.

How in the world did Arthur not notice this place was a mess? Was he partially blind? She'd have to keep an eye on him.

He may be a terrible housekeeper, but he did know how to cook. The eggs he made this morning had been very good. She guessed he had to fend for himself, except for the times Ida, the cook at the ranch next door, made food for him. She made a mental note to thank Ida for her generosity last night. The stew had been delicious.

Gwen made her way outside and stood on the porch. She noticed some movement in the barn yard and covered her eyes against the sun. She'd have to purchase a wide-brimmed hat when she had a chance to go to town. The only thing she had was a bonnet and it was hardly enough to shield her from the bright rays.

A whoosh past her skirts made her look down to see the small goat run behind her. She turned around and as she did the other goat appeared out of nowhere. They stared at her.

She stared back. "Don't you dare," she whispered.

They did. Both at the same time.

Her eyes got wide as the larger goat rolled over and down the three steps to land at the bottom, his legs straight out and stiff. His eyes were open and staring right at her.

Like it was her fault he fell!

The smaller goat rolled the opposite way behind where she stood. She looked to see if the thing was staring at her. It wasn't. She gave a look up to the clouds. This was so scary. These goats were not normal!

What in the world was she going to do?

She wasn't going to put up with this nonsense. This was her house and she wanted no shenanigans. "You two had better wake up right now and get out in the yard!"

As if on cue, they both rolled then stood straight up and stared at her. The larger goat had big, prominent eyes in high sockets. He was mostly black with some white spots on the front legs and under his belly. She reached out a hand and he came right to her, sniffing.

"Do you want something to eat?" she asked him, as if he'd answer back. She almost laughed at herself for the silly thought. "Well, let me get you a treat."

She turned to go inside. As she went through the door, she noticed her two visitors were right behind her. They walked through the door like they owned the place. She quickly turned. "Stop!" she ordered.

The smaller goat stopped, startled by her loud command. Gwen guessed the small goat was the girl since she didn't have horns like the other one did. The goat fell over and rolled before she stuck her legs straight out and laid still.

Instead of getting excited, Gwen laughed out loud.

She heard footsteps behind her. "I'm glad they didn't scare you this time."

Gwen turned to watch Arthur come through the door, a big smile on his face.

"I was prepared this time. It is actually kind of funny when they roll and it looks like they faint dead away."

"I find it amusing, too. Is the noon meal ready yet?"

Oh dear! Gwen had forgotten to prepare something to eat. He noticed her distress and held up his hand. "I'm now noticing all the work you've been doing. The place looks so sparkling clean. I hardly recognize it here. You've been so busy I'm sure you forgot to make anything. We can have eggs again. There is a basket full of them on the shelf."

Gwen wondered about the eggs since she didn't see any chickens roaming around.

"Let me see what I can put together. If you'd like to go out to the pump and wash up, I'll have something shortly."

He nodded, grinned and left through the front door. Gwen hurried to the kitchen, rummaging through the shelves. She found a few jars of canned jelly and set one on the table, carefully pulling the lid off and setting it aside. The jelly would taste good on the bread that was left over from last night. Then she got busy preparing a pan of eggs, her back to the table.

When she turned around, she noticed the jar of jelly was gone. After further investigation, which didn't take but a twist of the head, she saw why. The little female goat had quietly removed the jar from the table and was sticking her tongue in the jar licking the jelly. She had forgotten to give them a treat so the little one helped herself.

"Go on, shoo," Gwen told her. "That is not what goats eat." She didn't know exactly what they ate. She'd have to ask Arthur.

"What do we have here?" Arthur asked, returning from outside. "I believe this one ate the jelly. Look at the jar, it's half-way empty."

Gwen turned to the goat who was still standing in front of her, smacking her lips with her tongue. "Does she have a name?"

Arthur groaned. "Goats don't have names."

"Oh, yes they do." She turned to the little goat. "Your name is Jelly. Since you love licking the jar so much!" Gwen rubbed her ears and scratched her chin. The goat gave out a wavered cry.

"She likes you petting her," Arthur mentioned.

"You have goats and you didn't know this? Of course they love affection like anyone else."

"They are not my goats. They belong to the owner of the Bar M Ranch."

How did she know he was going to say that? The ranch owner seemed to own everything around here. "I guess you are right. Well, maybe they already have names."

"I don't think so. The owner never named them."

"How terrible. The man sounds like a monster. Is that what the M stands for. The Big Monster Ranch? I hope to never meet him."

She turned in time to find the larger goat watching her every move. Gwen swore he was waiting for her to give him a name. She stared back. The goat was fidgeting, moving his back legs slightly as if he was ready to go back outside but his job was to stay with Jelly. It was adorable and Gwen smiled when she anointed him with a name. "Sparky. Welcome to the Murdock farm."

"Sparky? You named him Sparky?"

"Yes. Sparky and Jelly."

Arthur grinned. "Well, Sparky. Take your lady outside, please. We are about to eat and I'm not sharing with you."

Gwen watched in amazement as Sparky nudged Jelly, who was still licking her mouth as she followed him through the door as if they understood Arthur's command. Arthur had a smile a mile wide. "They listened. Just like a child would," she mentioned, amazed at the two animals.

He gave her a look of victory. "When it comes time to raise our own, we won't have any problems."

She turned to the pan, not wanting him to see her blush as she thought about the way they'd have those children he was talking about.

Gwen had her back to him and began to dish eggs onto two plates. She heard a soft chuckle behind her and took a deep breath. The man was scaring the daylights out of her. He was so handsome and seemed to understand her nervousness.

But she didn't know if he would come to the marriage bed. Or, if she even wanted him too.

Chapter 6

"I can eat eggs all day long." Arthur wiped his mouth and threw his cloth napkin on the table. "I better get back to work."

Gwen gave him a strange look. "What is it you do out there all day?"

He sat back, trying to think of something brilliant to say. The fact was he had taken some bales of hay the ranch hands dropped off the other day and put them in the one stall that was being used by his mare. Most of the morning he spent sitting on said bales of hay wondering what to do next. He wasn't used to being idle, but he honestly didn't know what to do.

Arthur's gift was training horses. He loved to spend the day at his ranch breaking in new horses. Except he was lost now since he had to stay away and keep Gwen from the ranch. There were way too many men that worked for him who didn't know about the bet. They'd call him boss and it would be over.

He loved the everyday work of running a huge ranch. He had hired the best men to run his longhorn cattle division and he took care of breaking in the new horses, along with teaching others how. Here, he had no clue how to take care of such a small farm. If he were to be honest, the place was a disaster.

He had a feeling she knew it and wanted to discuss things with him. Does he get up and make his way to the barn to avoid the conversation or stay here and face the challenge of pretending everything is fine?

"I'd like to see the rest of the farm today if you have a few minutes to walk with me?" Her request was innocent. He noticed how shy she was, but saw a strength in the way she looked at him. He wanted to reach out and run his hand across her cheek, but he didn't.

Instead, he nodded. "Let me help you clean up and we'll take a walk." He busied himself cleaning up the mess the goat named Jelly had caused. While he was scrubbing the sticky floor, Arthur wondered how he was going to make her fall in love with him.

Looking around, he saw a dismal farm house in disarray. Her attempt at cleaning at least made things liveable. At least she hadn't run off first thing this morning. Most women in his circle of acquaintances would have been long gone by now. It's why he agreed to this silly bet. He had to constantly remind himself he was trying to win a bet, not make things worse by chasing her off. If he chased her off, he'd loose Henry and Lami and there was no way he was going to lose.

Which was now becoming a reality he hadn't expected. Gwen was taking this challenge as serious as he took training one of his horses. She had already scrubbed the house from top to bottom in one morning. Who does that except someone prepared to make a go of things?

That was a plus in his direction at least. He wanted to take a run to the ranch and brag to the other men that she was staying. At least for now. They still had the tour to get through. Would she stay after seeing the barn had one horse and the fields were barren?

"I'm all cleaned up and ready to go." Her soft voice made him aware that she was a full fledged woman and his wife. It had been so long since he had someone in his arms. He desired to hold her but shook himself. She was drawing him to her in a way he hadn't expected. This woman had only been here one day and she was starting to affect him in ways he hadn't thought about before. Until now. Until her.

He sighed. "I'm ready. After you." Arthur held the front door open while she walked through, a determination in her step he had noticed yesterday when she had marched across the yard to the house. It made him smile.

He strolled across the yard, ignoring the weeds that had overtaken the grass. "There isn't much to look at yet," he warned her.

Gwen peeked inside the barn before entering. "It's quite dark and drab in here. Why don't you open the other doors on the other side of the barn to let in some sunlight?"

He shrugged. "I only have one horse to house here. She doesn't need much light since she's out in the pasture most of the day."

"One horse? Where are the rest?"

"She is the only one I've acquired so far."

"Oh."

He nodded. "In time there will be more."

"I see. Can we look at the rest of the farm?"

"Certainly." He guided her to the corral where his mare was munching on overgrown grass.

"I suppose the corral houses one mare, also?"

"Yes."

"Do you have any cattle?"

"Not yet."

"I see."

"I will as soon as I save enough money."

"How do you propose to do that? You have no cattle to sell. You have no horses to train and sell. Do you have a milk cow?"

He shook his head. "I get my milk from the ranch next door."

"Chickens? I haven't seen any running around the yard."

Again, he hated to say the word. "No."

"How did we acquire the basket of eggs?"

"I, um,-'

"The neigboring ranch," she finished for him.

He nodded.

"I see."

"When does winter come in hard like I read about in the Pioneer Women's book?"

"You read a book to learn about life here? There is no book that will tell you the harsh truths of living through a winter here."

She stood facing him, hands on her hips. "Well, then, sir, why don't you explain how we are going to get through a harsh winter with no meat or milk from a cow, no eggs from chickens and fields that look as if they haven't been planted in years? There is no food stored in your kitchen to save a life!"

She had been taking a step closer with each word she spoke. Arthur was almost flush against her until her eyes widened and she realized how close she was. Her pale cheeks reddened and she quickly took a few steps back.

Arthur grinned. She had spunk! He had begun to worry at first because he was afraid she'd turn tail and head out of Dakota Territory as fast as the wind rushes through the tall pines.

He turned his back to her. He wanted her to stay. She was beautiful when angry and had the power to make him want to spend the rest of his life with her. How had that happened in one day? It was impossible to feel so strongly about someone when he had already made up his mind most women only wanted him for his riches! She seemed so different than all the others. The desire to keep her here was overwhelming.

Arthur let his shoulders slump in defeat. "I'm so sorry. You are right. We have nothing. I've brought you here on false pretenses." He turned dramatically around. "Gwen, I spent the last of my money to buy this piece of land. I begged the owner of the Big M Ranch, who owned this parcel, to spare me a few dollars, but he would not. He would not budge on full price."

"I'm starting to dislike the man or monster, whatever he is. I doubt I'll step one foot on his property. Ever."

"Good."

"Good?"

"He doesn't deserve to be in your presence. Not you, such a wonderful and kind person."

"Thank you," she said softly. She almost blushed again but turned away before he was able to see her reaction to his words. He could see she was starting to relax a bit. Maybe his cries for help would keep her here. He had to try for the sake of Henry and Lami. And him.

He stared at her, hoping his plea would be taken seriously. "I'm desperate, Gwen. I'll be totally honest. Most women want someone who has already established lands and is doing well. That's why I sent for a proxy bride instead of a mail order bride. A mail order bride would've turned around at seeing this place and ran far away. It wasn't fair to you. I'm sorry and I will allow you to leave right now if you want to."

He turned away, deliberately slumping his shoulders. Arthur stared at the ground, waiting for a reaction and sending little prayers to God up above his tactic worked. He needed her to stay.

"You've got to be kidding!"

There it was. She was going to up and leave and he'd lose his two prize possessions. He turned swiftly around to face her. "Answer me this at least before you go. If I were a rich man with a big cattle ranch like my neighbors, would you stay?"

Her jaw hung open. "How can you say that? If you were a rich man, we would not be standing here talking about how to get this farm in tip top shape! Would you really want to be someone like that monster up on the hill?"

Arthur almost cracked a smile, but held it back. He'd never been called a monster before. Most people liked and respected him. He was a hard worker, she just didn't know it yet. His big concern in all of this was he was lying through his teeth. How was she going to react when she found out the truth? "He's probably not as bad as I made him out to be. Honestly, he didn't have to sell this land to me. Even if it was originally my descendant's land three generations back." Looking at her huge eyes widening with anger, he realized maybe adding that part was too much of a dramatic flair.

"What! Your family once owned it and you had to buy it back at full price? That is absurd. Well, if I have anything to do with things around here, he will never step foot on this soil again." She crossed her arms over her chest, more angry at the rancher on the hill than at him. Maybe that was a good thing. He needed her sympathy right now to win that darn bet.

Arthur walked to her, taking her hands and holding them in his. "Gwen, I truly am sorry but I need your help. You are a hard worker and understand what has to be done here to make this a working farm. I promise you that if you stick with me and stay for sixty days to turn this around, I will give you ownership of this farm."

"What? How can you even say that? Everyone knows a woman can't own property when she is married."

"The contract says in sixty days we can annul the marriage if one of us wants to. If you agree to help me, I will give you the choice of freedom or to stay married to me. Either way, your name goes on the deed to this property. Then you can do what you want with it."

Gwen gave him a look that almost made him give up the farce and tell her the whole truth. He felt about two feet tall lying through his teeth. "Arthur, if you put the farm in my name in sixty days, that means you will have to give up your home. It makes no sense. Where will you go? Why would you do all this hard work just to give it up?"

"Because I realize that I have done you wrong asking you to come out here on false pretenses. You gave up your life in the big city for a lie. I can't possibly allow you to stay without giving you some kind of compensation."

"That's too much, I'm afraid." She let go of his hands and turned around to pace back and forth.

Arthur held his breath. She wasn't going to buy into his deal. His nerves were getting the best of him. He ran a hand over his brow. He grew his grandfather's ranch into what it was today because he had made good sturdy decisions. Why was this any different? "I can give you more. Name your price?" He felt ridiculous asking her to name a price. But, wasn't this what all women wanted? She had been put in a position to ask for whatever she wanted.

Except she was not like any other woman he knew. Her eyes flashed. "There is no price for my help, Arthur. I've agreed to marry you by proxy not knowing what I was getting when I came here. Now, you want to put a dollar sign on my help."

"I'm sorry. It's just most women would fail to see this situation as well as you do."

She didn't budge. "I will help you make this farm a working farm so we can live comfortably. I have nowhere else to go, Arthur. I've left my life in New York City and I will never go back to living in an overcrowded place where you have to struggle to get by unless you are wealthy."

"Truly?" Relief flooded through him knowing now he wouldn't lose his precious horses. Arthur wanted to race to the ranch and tell the others they lost. He probably didn't have to even pretend anymore. She just proved herself by showing him she'd stick around no matter what. He stood here in front of her like a pauper, a run down farm in the background and she was determined to stay anyway.

"Why wouldn't I, Arthur? Are we in this together or not?" She tilted her head when he didn't answer at first.

"Yes. Let's see if you mean those words. We still have almost sixty days to prove you can be a farmer's wife. According to the contract, either party can ask for an annulment by day sixty."

"What is there to prove, Arthur? I am already here and not planning to go anywhere."

He grunted. If his friends knew she had promised to stay no matter what, they were not going to make it easy on her. Well, he had to turn things around so they'd never find out. He wasn't their boss and the owner of the biggest cattle ranch in Dakota Territory for nothing. "You have nothing to prove, Gwen. But, perhaps I do."

She gave him another one of her strange looks that said she didn't understand what he meant. He hated to be so evasive but he didn't dare tell her about the bet they made. She was willing to stick around and help him build up the farm.

Now he knew what to do with it when their time was up. He had no intentions of keeping his name on this deed. He'd give it to her, lock, stock and barrel. Because he had a feeling when the truth of the matter came out, she was going to be angrier than a nest of hornets.

Chapter 7

Gwen wasn't surprised Arthur was penniless. She had known when she got here there was something wrong with this whole situation. When she looked in the barn there was one stall prepared for the mare. The rest of the stalls looked like they hadn't been used in a few years. She may not know much about farm life, but she did know there was no life that existed here other than their own.

Arthur showed her around the property. She was happy to see they did have a small spring house where the water stayed at forty degrees all year round. It was made of stone with a small wooden door, but it was big enough for her to get inside and look around.

"How did you get all this food?"

He shrugged. "Ida. She sends food down for me when I work at the ranch. I told you she thinks of me as a son. Besides, I can't refuse the poor woman. I do earn money, you know. I work for the monster two days a week breaking in horses."

"It can't pay all that much. He doesn't sound like he pays very well. I wonder how he keeps his help?"

"He does pay quite well for my skills as a horse trainer. I do have that in my favor. What others get paid is none of my business."

"At least when you get this farm up and running, you won't have to worry about him paying your wages. It will be nice to break all ties with such a man like him. You do plan to buy and train horses here, don't you?"

"I guess we can try. It is my dream. We'll have to fix the broken fencing before purchasing any more horses."

"I'd get started on that first. I will start to pull weeds in the yard and plant flowers. If you can take me to town, maybe we can purchase some flower seeds for next spring. I'd love to have some flower gardens."

"I'll have to earn a bit more money to buy those extras. Maybe in about three to four weeks we can."

He didn't seem to want to go to town. Arthur probably didn't have the extra dollars for a few seedlings. That was understandable if he was saving everything to buy cows and horses for his farm. "You are right. It is rude of me to assume we can afford such things yet. Do not worry, I have a solution."

He walked with her around the farm, showing her where the wood was kept in a covered shed. He pointed to a rattletrap of a wooden shed with wire over top of it, broken pieces sticking out. "Over there are some chicken coops but they will need repairs. It looks like some wild animal, probably a fox or wolf got in. I won't be able to bring chickens here until it is fixed. The chickens can roam the yard all day but at night need to be locked up."

She wondered what he had been doing all this time. "How long have you had this property, Arthur?"

Gwen noticed a muscle in his cheek twitched. "A week."

"Oh! No wonder nothing is done. I thought you had lived in this run down ram-shackle of a farm for a long time."

He stopped walking and laughed. "Run down ram-shackle? I see I haven't impressed you at all."

She gave him a pleasing smile. He was comical if anything. At least he didn't take her words too seriously. "I'm sorry, but I speak the truth when I see it. And this, sir, is quite a mess."

"Then it's up to the two of us to put it back in order."

"Do you know who lived here before you bought it?"

"An old, tired man. He was pretty sick from what I understand for a long, long time. It's why things were let go for so long. Everyone in the area, including me, thought his boys were staying with him to take care of him and found out too late it wasn't true. But when it came time for the old man to leave this earth, they had their hands out, ready to take the first offer of sale. It was a sad day."

"You make it sound like you were right there."

The muscle in his cheek twitched again. "I heard the story when I was at the ranch. The hands talked openly about it when it happened. That's how I found out about this place and made an offer to buy it from the ranch owner."

"You know quite a lot of the happenings at the ranch. What don't you know?" she asked, her curiosity getting the best of her. This man was quite intriguing. Gwen wondered what secrets he kept inside of him. He seemed to be an open book one moment and then the next time she looked at him, he acted so mysterious.

He took a step forward. "I know for certain a beautiful lady with the most beautiful dark brown eyes and skin so smooth is standing in front of me as if she is waiting to be kissed."

Gwen was mesmerized because that was exactly what she had been thinking. All she had to do was lift her chin and she'd be staring back at him. So she did. She wanted him to kiss her, too.

He was moving towards her. She raised her chin even higher and he caught her mouth with his own. Sparks flew the moment their lips touched. Gwen was quite shocked and didn't understand the fluttering in her belly or the blatant desire for this man that crept up through her whole body. She lifted her arms and placed them around his neck while he kissed her thoroughly.

Then he took a step back and stared into her eyes.

She was speechless. This was the best feeling in the word, but also a bit scary. What had just happened? Were they supposed to do this?

"I'm sorry. That was out of line." He truly looked sorry, but she felt differently. He hadn't been out of line. Not after that kiss, it was wonderful.

He turned away, breaking her hold on him. She let her arms drop to her sides when he turned back around as she spoke in a shaky whisper. "We are married. There is nothing wrong with a kiss between a man and his wife."

Then he did the greatest thing ever. He wrapped her in his arms and dipped his head for another kiss. She complied, unable to stop herself.

*****

Four weeks later Gwen was still thinking about that kiss. They had stood for so long holding each other while he kissed her like she'd never been kissed before. Then he had cupped her face in both his hands and smiled at her, a dazzling smile that she saw every night since as she lay in bed thinking about him.

He was sleeping in the barn, giving her time to get used to the marriage. At least that is what he told her. But, she had asked him to come to the house and at least sleep on the settee in the parlor. He refused and mumbled something unintelligible. She had let it go since he scooted out the door back to his safe haven.

For the past four weeks they had been working side by side outside. He hadn't allowed her to pick the weeds alone. The first day she had tried and barely put a dent in the yard. The next day he came along with her and began to work by her side. Before supper time, they had a quarter of the front yard cleared. By the end of the week the whole yard was weed free. Even the two days a week when Arthur went to work at the ranch, he still stopped in to check in on her. She found him an amazing man and such a hard worker.

They spent each evening having supper together, then they would retreat to the porch until the sun went down or go for a walk hand in hand along the property line. Arthur made her laugh at some of the things he told her about the horses he trained. There was one, a stallion he called him Henry, that he talked about quite often. Arthur planned to put him in a horse show someday if he ever had the chance.

"I think you'll be a great horse breeder. This farm is going to grow so huge you won't recognize it a few years from now."

He gave her a faraway look. "That would be nice," he told her.

She wanted to be a part of making his dreams come true but worried he wouldn't allow her to go into town. It would be nice to speak with other people now and again. Gwen had an idea about purchasing enough supplies to begin selling some baked goods. But she had to get to the mercantile to see if there was any interest in buying them.

Whenever she asked Arthur to take her to town, he claimed to be too busy. She tried again. "Is it possible to take a ride into town one day this week? I'd like to purchase some things. I have some money of my own I brought along."

He leaned over, his face close to hers. "Don't you know when you marry you have to hand over all your money to the man of the house?"

"What? I never heard that rule! Is it even a rule?"

He grinned.

She laughed. "You had me worried. I thought you were serious."

He gave her another look as if an idea just occurred. "Well, any extra money right now would help to buy some supplies for the winter. But, I'm not asking for any of your money."

Her face fell. The right thing to do was to hand it over so they had enough for the upcoming winter. What had she been thinking? Arthur was a man with a good, healthy plan. He knew what he was doing. She had just wanted to hurry him along because he deserved so much more. "I'll be right back."

When she came out of the bedroom, she held out her hand. "This is some money I had saved from my job in New York. I will be honest, I was worried that I'd get here and you'd be this horrible man who drank. From past experience, I wasn't about to be stuck here if something bad happened. Now I'm glad you are not a drinking man."

He stared at her hand.

"You aren't a drinking man, are you?"

He shook his head. "No. I despise drunkards."

"So do I."

He motioned for her to sit on the bench beside him. She sat down to face him. He hadn't taken her money so she held out her hand again. "Why do you hate drunkards? Please take this money. It will help us get through the winter."

When she looked into his eyes, they were so serious it made her sit back a ways.

He cleared his throat as if it was difficult for him to speak. "I can't take your money."

"Of course you can and you will. I'm not carrying it back to my room. If you don't take it, I'll throw it in the yard and Sparky and Jelly will eat the bills."

He looked around. "Where are they, by the way? I haven't seen them in a while."

Gwen smiled in triumph. "I made them a small bed in the barn. They now have their own space in one of the stalls. I even nailed up a sign with their names on it. They've been cuddling together ever since. I think I've seen them venture out once all day today."

When she insisted he take the last of her money, he did so reluctantly, a look of wonder on his face. Hadn't anyone ever given him something before? "Tell me why you hate drinking?" she pressed him.

He looked away and stared at the front yard. "My father began to drink when my mother died. He ruined our home, letting it go. Then he died of a broken heart or from drinking too much. I'm not sure which one."

Gwen touched his cheek. "I'm so sorry."

He shook himself. "It's in the past. No sense talking about it since there was nothing I could do as a young boy. I vowed never to drink like he had done. I don't associate myself with others who do."

"Good for you. My father is a drunkard. It's why I moved out of our family home. He also began when my mother died, but he remarried and it escalated from there. My step-mother is lazy and keeps buying him bottles to keep him inebriated while she spends his money. Sooner or later it will all come crashing down."

Arthur wrapped an arm around her shoulder while they both gazed at the sky filled with hundreds of sparkling stars. There were no words to exchange as they both were reminded how lucky they were to find a partner who wasn't tempted by the pleasures and curses of alcohol.

Gwen felt so lucky. Everything was going great. Even if she gave up all her money, she knew Arthur would never do anything to hurt her. He had proven to be a kind and loving man who cared about her feelings.

Everything was going to work out fine. They'd work and grow the farm until it was so huge they'd have to start hiring help. The way things were going, she couldn't imagine that anything could go wrong.

Chapter 8

Big M Ranch

Arthur stood in the center of the corral, waiting for the mare to allow him to get closer. He left her alone so she'd know he wasn't a threat. Then Harry, Walt and Edward showed up, causing her to side-step to the other side. The three men sat on the fence, their legs dangling over the side.

He strolled over to them knowing he wasn't going to make any more progress with the mare today. Arthur wanted to give her to Gwen. She was not quite as wild as the others had been. He figured she'd make a great companion for his wife.

"How's it going, Arthur? Has the wife fallen madly in love with you yet?" Harry was brutal when it came to teasing Arthur. They had known each other for far too long to treat each other any other way.

"I'd say that's none of your business. All you have to worry about is whether she'll be in love with a pauper in sixty days and with this charming face, how could she not?" He wasn't about to tell them she had already decided to stay with him. That was something they didn't need to know.

Walt gave him an appreciative look. "It sounds like things are going well for you, son. Maybe we should stir things up a bit."

Arthur stared down his foreman. "I didn't say they were going well. As a matter of fact, I didn't say anything at all except how can a woman not love a face like mine." His cheek twitched.

Walt stared at him like a father would to his son to see if he were telling the truth. The bad thing was Walt knew him way too well. He knew Arthur had always been straight up and honest every step of the way. Walt had been on the ranch when his father had almost destroyed it. There wasn't much that surprised the older man.

Now Arthur was worried. They knew him way too well. He had better make it sound like things were not going well. How was he supposed to do that when it wasn't true? Gwen was making life on that old dilapidated farm a pleasure, even if he didn't have a decent bed to sleep in. He was pretty sure it wouldn't be long until she'd allow that, but he had been the one holding off.

"Did you bed her yet?" Harry questioned in his brutally honest way.

"For crying out loud, Harry, that ain't none of our business!" Walt spit.

"Sure it is. We have a bet to win. It sounds like she's content living in that broken down farmhouse with our boss who should be here running his ranch. Instead, he's trying to win a bet."

"You're the one who suggested it in the first place."

"There ain't no woman alive who'd agree to live in that kind of squalor with Arthur!"

Arthur knew exactly what his best friend was doing. He knew Harry like the back of his hand. A grin formed on his face and he turned away before Harry realized he was on to him. The man was trying to test Arthur to see if he'd reveal what was going on. Arthur was too smart for that and Harry should know better. Even so, he wasn't telling these men a darn thing.

"There's still almost four weeks left to find out if I get to keep Henry and Lami or if you do. I'll tell you one thing, Harry. There is no way on God's green earth I'm giving up my prized horses."

"Not even for a woman you fall madly in love with?"

Arthur shook his head after a slight hesitation.

Harry stared him down, trying to read his face. "Oh, for Pete's sake, you fell in love already, didn't you, Arthur?"

Frustration rolled from Arthur's nostrils. His best friend knew him better than anyone. He was better off not coming to the ranch but he wanted to keep training his horses. "Our conversation is over. I'm taking Henry and Lami with me for a few hours. I'll bring them back later this evening."

He left the three men sitting on the fence while he saddled up the two horses. He got in the saddle and lifted his face upwards, thanking the God above for giving him so much. He didn't look at the men as he made his way to the end of the property line where his wife was working diligently to get the place ready for the winter.

He didn't tell her by winter time they'd be in a warm home and she didn't have to worry about too much snow or trying to stay warm. His home was equipped with everything she'd need, even an inside bath closet.

If anyone deserved to live in luxury, it was Gwen. She had proven to him over and over again that she'd stick with him. The only problem he foresaw was that he lied to her about who he was. When she finds out he is the monster on the hill, it may take awhile to get her forgiveness. Even so, he was prepared to do whatever it takes to keep her.

He'd do anything for his wife. Even give up his prized horses. Even so, he wasn't going to lose this bet yet. That wasn't his style.

He rode Henry across the field to their farm and stopped short to wait on Lami. He didn't have to hang onto her reins since she followed Henry. The two were inseparable.

Gwen had been getting a small garden ready for next spring. She was bent over with a rake when she looked up and saw him getting closer. She waved, then placed a hand on her back. As he got closer, Arthur realized how tired she looked.

All this time she had been taking this whole thing so seriously while Arthur and his friends were betting on her. She had nowhere to go if she left here. Would she even accept this property if he handed her the deed? She may be so angry at the fact they had a bet riding on her, she may walk away from it all. She was a determined woman. He wanted her as his wife forever, but he was also going to give her the choice of walking away if she wanted to. He hoped she didn't want to. Arthur was starting to feel ashamed that he had tricked her.

He tried to push those thoughts from his mind for now. He'd worry about it later. One thing he knew was she deserved to have a little rest and relaxation and he was going to make sure she got it today. "Gwen!"

"What do you have there?" She gazed up at him, the hat's wide brim covering her eyes to protect them from the bright sun. He had given her a new hat a few weeks ago to keep her pale skin from burning. She pushed it back and shaded her eyes.

"This is Henry, the monster's prized horse I trained."

Gwen walked up to the stallion and slowly began to run her hand along his mane. "You are quite a handsome boy." The horse let air out of his nostrils and lowered his head so she was able to reach up and scratch his nose. She giggled.

"Henry is my, er, is one of my favorites at the ranch."

She gazed at Arthur. "You look quite handsome sitting there, too." Then she blushed when she realized she spoke out loud. Her attention immediately went back to Henry and he didn't seem to mind at all.

Arthur grinned. He was in heaven right now. He slid from the saddle. "I'd like to introduce you to Lami. She's a gentle mare and my second favorite."

When Lami heard her name, she came up beside Arthur and nudged her nose under his hand. He leaned over and talked softly in her ear. "She's going to ride you today, Lami. Be gentle."

Lami seemed to understand. She lifted her head and looked right at Gwen, who had a frightful look on her face. "You want me to ride a horse?"

Arthur didn't realize she'd never ridden one before. "You need to learn if you want to live out here in the wilderness."

When Lami pushed her nose into Gwen's arm, she laughed and began petting the mare. Arthur stood and watched as they got to know each other. Lami knew she was nervous too and was trying to calm Gwen's fears. It was working, he could tell.

Finally, Gwen looked up. "Okay, I guess you are right. I should learn."

The next hour was spent showing Gwen how to get on and off a horse, how to sit in the saddle and how to lead Lami, even though she didn't need to be led. Lami was so dedicated to Henry, she'd follow him anywhere. Nothing would deter her from him. They were a match made in heaven.

"I think I'm ready to ride her out of the yard."

"Yes, you've done well, Gwen."

"What about the monster? Does he allow you to take these beautiful creatures off his property?"

Arthur gave her a grin. "What he doesn't know won't hurt him. He's out of town for a few days."

"Arthur! That's naughty of you." Even when she said it, he saw her face transform into a devilish smile.

It made him grin even more.

This was going to be an eventful day, he could already tell.

*****

Two hours later, they rode back to the farm after an exhilarating ride across the rolling hills. The days were starting to get shorter. Arthur hated to end their time together but he wanted to get the horses back to their stalls before it got too late. When they arrived at the farm, Sparky and Jelly were sitting patiently in the middle of the front yard like children waiting for their parents to come home.

Gwen jumped down from Lami like an expert. He was pleased she picked up so quickly after never having any experience riding before. That was his wife, determined, eager to learn and amazing in his eyes.

She reached in the pocket of her dress and pulled out a treat for the goats. He watched them both take it gently from her hand and walk away as if they had been waiting for the treat instead of her. Arthur knew this was too good to be true. Would she want to make a life with him? Maybe it was time to tell her the truth.

Except a small neigh rent through the air. He turned back to see Henry nodding his head. Arthur was torn. If he told her the truth now and she decided to leave, he'd lose these beautiful creatures.

He was sick and tired of deceiving her. He wanted to be honest. Although, when did honesty get him anywhere? He'd been truthful with every woman he'd ever met. Yet, they had all lied to his face, claiming to care for him, not his money. He'd been dead wrong every single time.

No, he had to be absolutely sure with Gwen. But, wasn't he? To look at how hard she worked each and every day told him one thing; she didn't care how rich he was. She even gave the last of her money to him.

She did it because she was his wife and wanted to make his dreams of owning a horse ranch come true. No one in his circle would ever do such a thing. Arthur sighed. He had to force himself to wait for another thirty days before he told the truth. He had spent time and money making Henry and Lami into two of the best horses anyone had ever seen. They were the beginning of a breed the Big M Ranch would be proud to own.

He was torn. What mattered more?

Chapter 9

Gwen busied herself in the kitchen while she waited on Arthur to come home. She hoped he was not going to get into trouble taking the two horses from the ranch, but secretly glad because they had such a wonderful day. She was gleaming from the day of riding and spending hours with Arthur.

The future was looking brighter each day. She imagined they would be able to buy horses he could train by next spring if he kept working through the winter. In their conversation today, Gwen found out there was a small town even closer than Green River or Bryan. It was not huge by any means but most of the ranches in the area got their supplies there.

Dakota Falls was about a thirty minute ride from here, Arthur told her. There was no railroad there so the businesses had to haul their goods and services by wagon from the other larger towns like Green River or Bryan. He said maybe a hundred people lived in town, mostly men. Everyone within a fifty mile radius went to Dakota Falls for supplies.

Gwen saw the potential for making extra money after Arthur told her how there were not many women there. Why not supply something to these hard working men she knew they would love? Something mouth watering, like her special chocolate chewy cake.

She had concocted a chocolate cake one day, using cocoa and slivers from a chocolate bar. In New York City, chocolate bars were in all the small shops. Somehow Gwen had been distracted and forgot to add the baking powder. The cake came out half the size and so chewy and delicious it made everyone's mouth water.

It had taken her a long time to figure out where she had made the mistake, but in the meantime, her friends ate up the cake like they had been starving. If she could sell her mouthwatering cake to the men in Dakota Falls, maybe he'd be able to buy at least one horse before winter set in.

But, she had to show her husband it was possible first before he'd agree to anything. It was a way to help him succeed much sooner. She'd do a test run and prove it was possible first.

Since she had learned to ride a horse today she was going to talk to Arthur this evening about teaching her to drive the wagon. If the supply town was only thirty minutes away, she'd be able to go herself. That way, she didn't need to explain what she was doing. It would be a complete surprise to him and she'd prove it was possible to accomplish.

All she needed was one day on her own to prove her idea was a good one. She saw Arthur as a man of action and yet when it came to her, he was so adamant about her not going to town. So, she'd have to show him she was fine on her own.

She fixed their evening meal, leftover stew from yesterday, and took the surprise dessert from the oven. Gwen had made a double batch since she had plans for the rest. Setting the table, Gwen became more excited about her idea. If she was able to earn money selling her chocolate concoctions to the men in Dakota Falls, then she'd be able to buy a horse and make payments from a steady income.

But, first she had to find out how much a horse would cost.

Arthur's footsteps on the porch made her smile. When he came inside, the hair along his neckline was wet where he had washed his face and hands. "Sit down," she ordered, then went to fill their plates with stew.

"What is that incredible smell?" he asked, raising a brow. Gwen had made some delicious baked goods before so it really wasn't a surprise for him to come home to find a dessert on the table.

"You can taste it after we eat," she told him, nodding towards the plate. They gave thanks and ate, all the while she was excited to see what he thought about her dessert.

Finally, he pushed back his plate. "I'll have that dessert right now."

She sliced a piece of the cake and set it in front of him. He dug in, the fork disappearing into the chewy chocolate. She watched as he closed his eyes and chewed on the cake. He didn't say a word.

She was crushed. "Do you like it?"

He opened one eye, then the other. "Mm."

"Is that good?"

He laid the fork down and picked up the rest of the cake, then shoved it into his mouth. Her eyes got huge. Then she threw her head back and laughed. He loved it!

After he ate the whole thing in practically one bite, he wiped his mouth and gave her a long kiss, crumbs on his mouth and all. "That was the best cake I've ever eaten. Why, you could cut them in squares and sell them, that's how good it is!"

Gwen didn't say a word. She knew right then her chocolate mistaken cake would be a hit with the townsfolk of Dakota Falls.

They retired to the porch to watch the sun go down. Usually, they held hands. Tonight was no different. "Arthur?"

"What is it, Gwen?"

"Will you teach me how to hook up the horse to the buggy so I can learn everything there is to know about this farm? I think that's about the only thing I don't know how to do."

"You did learn to ride today. I'd like to spend more time showing you how to care for a horse, brushing him, cleaning out the stalls sometime."

She wrinkled her nose. "I'd really like to learn how to hook up the wagon."

He frowned. "Are you trying to run away from me? Once you know how to hook up the horse and buggy, I may come home to find you gone."

"How can I do that when you have to take the mare to the ranch when you leave here since we only have one horse?" She was wondering herself how she was going to go into town if he had the mare. Maybe she could drop him off with the pretense she was going to practice.

"Ah, good point. I'll tell you what. Since learning to drive a horse and buggy isn't something you can learn in one day, I'll show you tomorrow how it's done. Then on Friday, you can drop me off at the Big M property line and I'll ride Henry home later in the afternoon."

It was a perfect plan and she was so glad he suggested it so she didn't have to. "Is the monster still out of town?"

"He comes and goes. But, I'm sure on Friday he won't be there."

"Are you sure you don't mind? I'd really feel better being here alone all day if I know each and every job."

"You are right. I married a very smart, honest and caring woman."

She smiled. "You have excellent taste."

He lifted her hand and kissed the back of it. "Seems I do," he bragged.

She leaned back into the chair watching the sun go down. He was so perfect, just like the setting sun.

*****

On Friday morning, she dropped Arthur off at the property line where he had wanted dropped off. "Are you sure you don't want me to drive you to the ranch?"

He shook his head. "I'm afraid you need to practice a bit more, Gwen. Take the wagon around the yard and maybe up and down the lane but don't go out on the road yet. I'll drive with you on the road just to make sure."

"Make sure of what? I'm doing great and you know so!"

She was certain he was stalling her by insisting she wait to go anywhere without him. Gwen felt pretty confident she'd have no trouble taking the buggy to town. Yesterday she had even drove down the road some to make sure. Now, she was ready to get back to the farm house and get on with her task.

He turned and waved several times as he made his way up the rolling hill towards the monster's ranch. Gwen watched him go over the crest and turned the buggy back to the house. There, she loaded the wagon with her goods. Gwen had spent half of the day yesterday hitching the horse and buggy, practising until she felt confident and then she made two more pans of her cakes in between all of that.

After they cooled, she cut them into long bars, covered the pans and set them on the floor of the buggy. She lifted the rifle from the wall in the parlor and set it underneath the seat of the buggy.

Gwen rode away from the farm and took a right at the end of their drive. She knew the town wasn't to the left since that took her past the Big M Ranch. Besides, she hadn't seen any small towns on her way here the first day they came.

The ride was actually nice and peaceful as she passed more rolling hills and open land with huge mountains in the background. Some areas were lined with tall pines that closed the road like a narrow path. Then she'd see open fields and hills that seemed to go on forever.

There was a chill in the air but nothing she wasn't getting used to. The thought of buying herself a warmer coat occurred to Gwen as she drove towards Dakota Falls. Perhaps she'd see what the cost of one was and speak to Arthur about it.

That made her smile. She was deliberately going behind his back and against his wishes to earn extra money to purchase another horse for the farm. Yet, she wanted to ask him if there was money to buy a winter coat. Shaking her head at her own silliness, she almost missed the small wooden sign that read Dakota Falls, you are here.

If she was here, there was nothing at all in front of her but a bunch of tall pines blocking both sides of the road. She drove past the trees and went through a sharp curve to find the road lined with buildings on either side.

Dakota Falls! It was a small town indeed. Arthur did say one hundred people lived here so she figured it was enough to get her chocolate business started. She found the mercantile and pulled up front, tying the rawhide straps to the post since she wasn't too confident the mare would listen and not wander away.

She leaned over and took both trays into the store. Rows upon rows of merchandise stuffed into every crevice and overloading the shelves made it hard to even find the counter. "Hello?" she called out, worried she wouldn't be able to find the proprietor in all this mess.

"Straight ahead until you see the row of bonnets, then take a left," a voice called out.

Gwen followed his instructions, weaving through the rows. How was anyone going to be able to find her desserts in this chaotic mess? When she got to the counter, which was actually cleared off, she set the two trays there.

A large man, his hair thinning on top and hair that stood out over top his ears gave her a pleasant smile. "What do you have here?"

"Hello. My name is Mrs. Gwen Murdock and I'd like to know if you would be interested in buying my desserts to sell in your store?"

He nodded towards the covered pans. "Names Fred Folger. They smell good. Let's take a look."

"I have a sample for you right here." She lifted the cover and produced a small piece for him to taste.

Besides his eyes rolling back in his head, he gave every indication he'd like to buy them. "How much?" he asked.

"I'd like ten cents a piece. There are twelve bars in each pan."

He stared at her. "Doesn't Murdock have enough money? He's got you out selling cakes? Heck, I didn't know he got shackled."

Before she could reply, a female voice from the back room called out. "Father, can you come help me, please?"

"I'll be right there," he called out. Fred turned back to Gwen. "I'll give you five cents a piece."

She shook her head, his comment about her husband's money forgotten, determined to get the highest price. "They are worth ten cents." As she spoke, she heard the bells jingle on the front door.

Voices were heard behind her as she was haggling prices with the shop owner.

She turned around to find two men behind her. Gwen picked up another sample piece, tore it in half and handed each man chocolate. They thanked her and moaned while they ate the dessert.

She stared at Fred, proving that they were worth ten cents.

"How much, miss? I'll take another one."

"Do you think they are worth twenty cents?"

"I'd pay twenty-five," the one man announced. She turned back to Fred, her brow raised, waiting for him to make a decision.

Fred chewed on his bottom lip, then rubbed his stubbly chin. "I don't know."

"I can open my own shop. I passed a few empty buildings on my way here." She had no intention of doing so but knew how to bluff.

The shop owner gave her a hard look. "I'll pay you ten cents a piece." He dug in his register and gave her the money, then retreated to the back when the female voice called out again.

"Thank you, gentlemen. If you want more, you'll have to buy through Mr. Folger's store. I hope you tell everyone about these Chocolate cakes."

They both tipped their big hats and promised to spread the word. Hopefully, in a week she'd be able to come back with more. She had an idea and looked for a sign that told her where the livery was located.

"I'd like to put this money down on a horse," she told the man standing in front of her.

"I don't recognize you, ma'am. We can't extend credit to strangers."

"My name is Mrs. Gwen Murdock. I live a half hour from here and would like to buy an extra horse. How much do they cost?"

"Your talking about one hundred fifty dollars. How much you got there?"

She counted out her profits. "Two dollars and forty cents. That's just the beginning. I'll have a payment for you each week. By the way, if you want some good sweets, go to the mercantile and ask for the Chocolate cakes."

"Chocolate cakes?"

"Yes, sir. I sell them at the mercantile. As a matter of fact, I just dropped off two pans full. You may want to get some before they are sold out."

"We never have sweets! Okay, I'll do this only because you say you are a Murdock. If you are pulling my leg, I know Mr. Murdock will make it right. So, I'll take that deposit and you can have your pick of one of the horses in either of the stalls on the right. Here, sign this." He opened a book and scribbled something Gwen wasn't able to decipher. His writing was atrocious, but she signed her name before he slammed the book shut. "I'll be back."

Gwen wandered over to the two stalls to decide which horse she wanted. They were both solid but there was something about the gray mare that made her pause. She was awfully fat. "It looks like someone has fed you way too much feed." The other mare was a pretty brown and white, but the more she petted the gray mare, her decision became clear.

When the stable owner came back, his hand filled with two of the cakes, she gave him a huge smile and let him know which one she had chosen. "I'll tie her to the back of the buggy and take her along with me."

"Make sure you feed her a little extra," he told her, his mouth so full of chocolate she barely made out a word. He threw a bag of grain onto the back of her buggy. "I'll even throw in some free food."

She waved and began to head out of Dakota Falls, completely satisfied she made the right decision. As she went past the mercantile, the owner poked his head out the front door. "When are you coming back again?"

"Next week."

"Bring double what you did today. I've got one pan sold already."

She nodded and left the town behind, anxious to get back home.

Home. It was a nice thought. No longer closed in by tall buildings or smoggy air, the mountainous ridges and peaks were a much better sight to see. Gwen was feeling quite impressed with herself when she pulled the buggy up to the front porch.

Henry was in the corral when she untied the gray mare. Stroking her mane, the dark eyes gazed into her own. They looked so sad it almost made Gwen cry. "I'll take care of you, I promise. That will be your name. Promise. You will be so happy here."

She let the mare into the corral with Henry, who sniffed her a few times then continued to eat grass. Promise stayed on the opposite side almost as if she were afraid to move. Had someone been cruel to her?

Gwen turned around to see a silhouette of a man in the door of the barn. Arthur stood there, hands in his pockets. She hurried towards him, excited to show him what she'd done when she stopped short.

He didn't look happy.

No, he did not. Not at all.

Chapter 10

Arthur was too angry to speak. Gwen was running towards him, holding her skirts in the air and a smile on her face as if she hadn't disregarded his wishes and went to town on her own. He knew that's where she went because two of his men told him about a lady using his buggy to sell chocolate cake.

The chocolate cake she made for him!

"Arthur? Why are you looking at me that way? You look so angry."

A moment ago she was ecstatic. Now, she looked confused and he was the one who caused it. But, right now he didn't care. She was going to mess everything up. Didn't she understand he was about to lose Henry and Lami if she found out about the bet before the sixty days were up? "I came here to check up on you and wasn't able to find you anywhere."

She gave him an apologetic look. "I'm sorry. I did go behind your back, Arthur. Can I tell you why?"

He was trying hard to keep it together. His hands were shoved in his pockets and he clenched his fists together. "Why don't you tell me why?"

She tried to get closer but he pulled his hand from his pocket and held up his hand. "No. Please explain, Gwen."

Her face fell. She looked more worried now. He didn't want to be so hard on her, but didn't she understand his prized horses were at stake? Of course she didn't know. What was he thinking? She had him so confused.

"I wanted so badly to help you start your horse farm. I thought since you loved my chocolate cakes so much I'd be able to sell them at the mercantile, and I was right. Fred Folger bought them for ten cents a piece. At first he told me five cents, but these two ranch men came in and I gave them a sample. When they said they'd pay twenty-five cents, the mercantile owner changed his mind and gave me what I wanted."

"I told you to wait for me to take you to town, Gwen. Why didn't you wait?"

She sighed, looking him in the eye. "I've lived on my own for three years after I left my family home, Arthur. I think I'm adult enough to make a few of my own decisions."

She was right. He had no business holding her back except for the fact he didn't want her to find out that he had deceived her. Now the truth had to come out.

She took him by the hand and he walked with her to the corral. "See what I bought for you?"

"A pregnant mare?"

Gwen gave him a sharp look. "A what? Pregnant? Oh, dear!" She slid between the two wooden slats to check on the mare. "No wonder you look frightened. It's because you are."

"She looks like she is about to go into labor."

"The man at the livery didn't mention she was pregnant."

"He wouldn't, but it's a wonder he didn't charge you more for her."

"He was too obsessed with my chocolate cakes. He bought a handful."

"I have to admit, you are quite a salesman."

"Sales woman. Now what?"

"We wait."

"Do we need to call a doctor?"

"No. I can help her if she has any trouble."

"That's true. You are familiar with horses. She is yours, Arthur. Her name is Promise."

Arthur ran a hand down her mane. "She's a good, sturdy horse. What am I supposed to do with her?"

"Train her. You said you wanted a horse farm. This can be the beginning of one. I'm going to pay her off with the sale of my cakes. Fred Folger wants double the cakes next week. That means I can make a double payment on Promise."

Arthur frowned. "How much did Percy White charge you for her?"

"He said a good horse runs about a hundred fifty dollars."

Arthur made some noise under his breath. He turned to Gwen. "Please, let me do the horse buying from now on. You probably paid about fifty dollars too much for her. The other problem is she is already trained. I train wild horses, Gwen."

Gwen's bottom lip quivered as she tried to maintain her dignity. "I am sorry. I did not know."

He gathered her in his arms. "It's why I asked you to please let me go with you when you venture out and about. I realize you were only trying to help. I love you for that."

She lifted her head and stared at him. "Did I hear you just now?" Her words were whispered.

He didn't realize he said it out loud. How was he going to handle this? He did love her but he didn't want her love on false pretenses any more. It was time to tell her the truth no matter what happened. "Look, Gwen, we have to talk about -"

The loud noise the mare made had them both running towards her. She dropped her front legs to her knees and began to call out with a distressed sound. Gwen looked at him for guidance.

"You stay with her. I'll go put Henry in the barn so he doesn't get spooked." He secured Henry in a stall that had been cleared earlier in the week while Sparky and Jelly looked up at him from across the barn. They were settled in their space happy as two goats can be. Not even the noises from a laboring mare were going to get them riled up.

It was going to be a long night. Something wasn't right with the mare. Or, Promise as Gwen called her. He left Henry in the barn and went back out to Gwen, who was whispering to the mare and crying. It looked like Henry would have to spend the night at the farm.

He knelt down beside her and saw his wife's tears. "Don't cry, Gwen. She's fine." But, after a few hours, the mare was still in distress with no foal on the way. He decided to take a look and see if he could help deliver.

It took most of the night with the two coaxing the mare to give birth, when Arthur helped it along, pulling on legs that were breached. "She's coming out backwards, but she'll make it," he told Gwen.

Six hours later, they had a beautiful golden foal lying beside her mother on the ground. Promise was exhausted but they both pushed her to force the baby to get up. Twenty minutes later the foal stood on shaky legs. It was a beautiful thing to see.

Gwen leaned her head on his shoulder. They were both exhausted. "Let's get these two in a stall and wash up. Daylight will be in a few hours. We need to get some sleep."

It didn't take much effort to get Promise and the foal to go inside. Henry was snorting but he was adapting to the small space he had to put up with. The two goats were curious, getting up from their comfortable spot to inspect the new foal. After a few sniffs, and Promise standing in the way, Sparky and Jelly went back to their cozy corner.

Gwen leaned against the well as she washed her arms and face. At one point, Arthur thought she was going to fall over. He took a towel and dried her arms and cheeks, then lifted her in his arms and carried her inside.

She fell asleep in his arms. He laid her on the bed and covered her with a blanket from the bottom of the bed. He almost laid beside her. The bed looked so inviting but he knew it wouldn't be right. Arthur sighed and went back out to the barn, finding solace in a soft bed of hay. He needed to be out there in case one of his horses needed him. At least that's what he told himself.

*****

For the next two weeks, Gwen watched the foal grow with the help of Promise. Each Wednesday she baked her chocolate cakes and Thursday morning she hitched the buggy and made the short trip to town. Arthur had been busy with Henry he said, staying at the ranch next door almost every day.

He'd come back at supper time and they'd eat together before sitting on the porch to watch the sun go down. Some evenings they walked to the corral to see the foal carry on. She was going to be a beautiful mare, like her mother.

"I'm off to Dakota Falls, little one. I still haven't found the perfect name for you. I hope you don't mind." Her eyes lit up. "Hope. That's your name." Satisfied, she carved out the word on a small piece of wood and attached it to the foal's stall. The barn was starting to fill up.

Each day, Arthur rode Henry or Lami to the farm, putting them up for the night. When she questioned him he told her the monster was okay with allowing him to do so. She thought that awful odd considering the man was so mean. "I hope you aren't going to get into trouble," she told Arthur but he just shrugged. There was something bothering him and she wasn't sure what it was.

She had tried to speak with him but he hurried away as if he had more important things to do. Either he had to check on Henry, or the mare, or he forgot something from the barn. He'd take off before they got into a deep conversation. Even the evenings on the porch were different.

He no longer held her hand or gave her a kiss. Almost like he was pulling away from their relationship. She had been about to tell him that she wanted to be his wife in more than name only when he began to act so strange.

Gwen sighed, steering the buggy towards the mercantile. She missed her friends from New York. She had sent a letter to Bessie but never heard back yet. It would be nice to be able to have a girl talk, especially since she was so confused at Arthur being so aloof lately.

"Do you have four pans this time?" Fred Folger had seriously been selling more and more each week. The men in Dakota Falls were loving the cakes.

"I do and I have a personal one for you." She knew Fred had bought a few of the cakes himself because his wife had died a few years ago. He had no one to cook or bake for him except his daughter, who worked at the Big M Ranch. He said she stopped in every week to buy supplies but she never baked him cake like this.

When she dropped off the cakes, she was about to leave when Fred's daughter stepped out from the back room. She was a beautiful woman, around the same age as Gwen with perfectly kept blonde hair and the bluest eyes. Her high cheeks and pale skin would make a man look twice. "Hello," she said to Gwen, looking a bit surprised to see her here. "So you are the owner of these delicious cakes?"

"Hello, and yes, I'm Gwen. Nice to meet you."

"It's a pleasure to meet you. I'm Ida Folger."

The name stopped Gwen in her tracks. "Did you say Ida?"

The woman blinked a bit too fast. "Yes, I am Ida."

"You work at the ranch next to my farm?"

She nodded. Her face once friendly became cautious. Gwen noticed. Was she in love with Arthur? Was that why she sent all that food along with him to the farm? If she was, Gwen was about to put a stop to it right now. "Well, you certainly do not have a limp or gray hair in your advanced age."

The two women stared at each other. Ida motioned to Gwen. "I think we should go across the street to the café and have some tea."

Gwen thought it was a grand idea since she planned to get some answers before she left Dakota Falls today. "I'd love to."

Chapter 11

Arthur was going to tell her the whole truth the moment Gwen returned from Dakota Falls. He had taken Henry and Lami both out for a last ride this afternoon, knowing he'd be giving them up. It had been a good run with the both of them. They had been wild horses at one time and he loved them like he'd love his own children some day.

The thing was, he loved Gwen more. She had given him a new lease on life these past few weeks. And all he had done was deceive her from the start while she tried to make this a home. He never felt more defeated then he did this very moment. Arthur didn't believe in giving up and he sure didn't want to now. But, if he had to prove anything to himself, then he knew the right thing to do was to decide who was more important in his life. Or, what was more important? A bet, or Gwen?

It was a terrible bet that he went along with, yet at first he had wanted to win so badly. But when it came down to living like this for another week and a half deceiving the woman he loved, Arthur knew he had to end the farce.

Gwen was now an independent woman. Through her ingenuity, she was now able to make her own living selling her chocolate cakes. Whether she knew it or not, she had never needed anyone. But he'd sign the farm over to her after he told her the truth. Then she'd be able to do with it as she wished.

He ached inside knowing she'd have a choice to stay or leave. He wanted her to want to stay with him, but he knew she had to make the choice when she learned the truth. It was all up to Gwen.

Leading the two horses, he walked over to the far side of the corral where the three men were working. Harry had his back to him and turned around when Arthur walked up.

"What's going on, Arthur?" He gazed over at Henry and Lami. "Is something wrong with them?"

Arthur handed over the reins. "You won. Henry and Lami are no longer mine." He looked each man in the eye. "The bet is over. This whole thing backfired on me. I fell in love with Gwen."

"Come on, Arthur. You have all but two weeks left. Play this out. I hear she's working hard to make that farm a happy little home, even selling her cakes in town. Why, she'll make a great wife." Walt piped in, knowing how much the two horses meant to him. "Don't give up yet."

Arthur shook his head. "I'm not giving up, Walt. I'm choosing. I want Gwen. But, I lied to her and now I have to make it right. Hopefully, she'll still have me after I tell her the truth."

Walt gave him a knock on his shoulder. "You're doing the right thing, Arthur."

He nodded. With a heavy heart he took one last look at his prized horses and turned his back on them. There would be more. He'd probably have plenty of time to break in new horses after Gwen walked away.

"Uh, Arthur?"

He stopped when Edward spoke up. He was usually the quiet one. "What?" Arthur turned in time to see the two younger men speaking in low tones. "What's going on?"

Harry stepped forward. "I think you probably want to hurry back to the farm and let Gwen know you don't really have a ten year old son."

"Say what?"

Harry shrugged, but his brow was creased with worry. "Well, we figured Gwen was falling for you and had to put a dent in things. We didn't want to make it so easy on you. After all, we had two champion horses to win."

Arthur strolled across the yard until he was about two inches from Harry. "What did you do?"

Harry stepped back. "We sent Ida's cousin's boy to the farm to pretend he was your son."

Arthur cursed under his breath. He shook his head. "She'll never believe it!"

Walt laughed. "I didn't know about this, Arthur. I wouldn't have agreed, although it has to be comical."

Arthur glared at his foreman. "There is nothing funny at all about this. This may ruin any chance I may have had to keep the woman I love!"

"We're not keeping your horses, son."

Arthur frowned. "What do you mean? A bet is a bet."

"We were hoping you'd find true love and it worked. We never had any intention of keeping Henry or Lami. They are yours and the bet is void."

Harry and Edward both agreed.

"You got me into a mess! I'm taking Henry." Arthur all but leaped onto his stallion and raced towards the farm. He had to get there and clean up the mess his hired hands and best friend made.

*****

Gwen pulled the buggy into the yard, unhitched the wagon and led the mare to the corral. She gave Ellie a good brushing before walking back to the porch. She had to smile at Promise and Hope. They had been exhausted for a few days but now were spunky and ready to run. She wanted to ride Promise but knew it would be awhile.

A pony and cart was coming down the lane at full breakneck speed. Gwen began to hurry across the yard to find out what was wrong. No one ever came down their lane.

The buggy stopped. A young woman with dark hair drove the buggy and a small boy who looked to be about ten years old jumped from the seat. He was holding a small bag. "You tell him it's his turn now. I've had him for ten years and he needs a father's hand. The boy won't listen and talks back too much."

The woman jumped down, gave the boy a hug and got back on the wagon. "You tell him he knows where to find me."

"How much did they pay you?"

The woman's eyes went so wide, Gwen could see the whites from where she stood. "I beg your pardon?"

"How much did they pay you to pretend this boy is Arthur's son?"

"He is Arthur's son."

"I'll pay you double."

"Double? Truly?"

"Yes, but you have to tell me who put you up to this?"

She bit her bottom lip then revealed everything. "It was Harry, Arthur's best friend. I was told to drop him off and what to say. I don't know what all is going on, but I heard them talk about testing you to see if you'd run or stay. They said this would truly be a good way to test you."

Gwen didn't know if she wanted to laugh or cry. She wasn't sure if his friends were interfering or crazy! "Is this your son?"

The woman shook her head. "No, he is Ida's cousin's child. We told her he was staying at the ranch to learn to ride a pony."

"Do you work at the ranch?"

"Yes, my name is Martha. Edward talked me into going along with this but he said it was for Arthur's good. I'm sorry."

"Martha, I'll have my husband settle with you tomorrow. The boy may go home with you."

She nodded, happy to get the boy and leave. "What do I tell Edward, Walt and Harry?"

"Tell them I am not going anywhere and they'd better keep their eyes open after I settle in there."

"Yes, ma'am." The boy sat beside her, his head down.

Gwen got closer, lifting his chin so he had no choice but to look at her. "Would you like to ride a pony tomorrow?"

He nodded, his eyes getting brighter. She even saw a smile. "Okay, you will have a pony ride. I'll have Arthur personally take you on one."

Arthur was going to work hard at redeeming himself. She gave a long, cool smile to the woman and waved as they went flying up the road towards the ranch.

She turned just in time to see Henry galloping across the pasture, then watched in fascination as he jumped the fence separating the two properties. Gwen crossed her arms and waited.

Arthur brought the horse to a quick stop, slid from the saddle and marched over to her. "Gwen?"

She wasn't about to let him off the hook so easily. He had to see the buggy leaving. "Hello Arthur."

"Who was that?"

She placed a hand on his cheek and laughed out loud. "Oh, you won't believe the day I had. That was a young boy who claims you are his father. The woman was going to dump him off here and I simply put my foot down. I told her that you have no such son. If you did, you'd have told me about him. Am I right?"

Arthur stood frozen, turned to her and started to open his mouth when she went on. She wasn't going to give him any time to respond. "Anyway, don't answer that, of course I am. You'd never hide something like that from me." She stepped away from him, turned towards the barn so her back was to him.

"Listen, Gwen," he choked out, his voice low.

She waved her hand in the air, forcing herself to keep from turning around. "I was in town and guess who I met? You won't believe it! Ida, the monster's cook! We had tea together. Of course, I had to help her across the street since her limp was so awful she had a hard time even walking. That poor, poor old woman. I think I should go help her now and again, volunteer my services since she has a hard time of things. How can that monster take advantage of the aging woman?"

He made a noise but she didn't dare turn to see his face. Gwen tried hard not to turn around. She was actually enjoying herself.

Now, to throw in a few more little white lies. See how he liked this one.

"Then, because of her advanced age, I gave her a ride back to the ranch since the other ranch hands left without her. Why haven't you taken me there before? It's a beautiful place. I'm so envious of the woman who will eventually run the home there."

"Gwen," he croaked.

She kept on, pretending not to notice he was trying to speak. "You may want to take some pointers from that monster. He must be a horrible person but look at all the riches he has. Why, if I had married a man like him, I'd be living in the lap of luxury instead of this old ram-shackle of a house!"

He made another noise again, this time it sounded different. She swung around, ready to lay into him for deceiving her. When she turned and faced him, he was trying not to laugh out loud. She put her arms around his neck and gazed into his eyes.

He laughed then, his eyes crinkling at the corners. She truly loved this man who had spent the last six and a half weeks staying in a run down farm for her and sleeping in a barn.

"Who told you?" he asked.

"Ida. We accidentally met at the mercantile. When I realized she was not old with a lame foot, my suspicious mind was set straight. Ida knew it was time to fill me with the details of a certain bet that was made. We had a nice long conversation over tea."

He wrapped his arms around her and pulled her close. "I'm so sorry, Gwen. I don't even know how I got talked into this mess."

"I'll have to admit I was angry at first. I wanted to come back here and pack my bag and leave it all behind. But then I realized we had worked so hard together to make this work. It wasn't about being lied to or winning a bet. It was about us. You and me. I hope you have found that I don't care about riches, Arthur."

"I knew a few weeks ago where your heart was. The day you handed me the last of your money, I knew then you were in this for the long haul. After that I started realizing not even Henry and Lami were as important to me as you are. I love you, Gwen."

She shivered in his arms. "I love you, Arthur. I'm sorry we will have to leave this place. It's cozy and warm."

"I'm sure when you stay at the ranch for a few days, you won't miss this place at all."

As if on cue, Sparky and Jelly came across the yard like they were afraid to be left behind. She leaned over and scratched Sparky behind the ears. "Don't you worry, everyone is going with us. You, Jelly, Promise, Hope and of course Henry."

"They had no intention of letting me give up my prized horses. It was all a ruse to help me find the right woman."

She smiled. "Did you find her?" She wrapped her arms tighter around him. He pulled her close.

"I sure did. And I'll never let her go."

"Amen to that. Can we stay here tonight? I'd rather have you all to myself before we go to that busy ranch."

Sparky and Jelly made a few more noises and then walked back to their pen. "I'll be right back. Don't go anywhere," Arthur ordered.

She watched as he slid the saddle from Henry's strong back and put him in the barn for the night. He called in Promise and Hope and Gwen smiled as they followed his lead into the barn. After he locked up, Arthur came across the yard like a man on a serious mission.

She squealed when he picked her up in his arms, then strolled across the yard, kicking the front door open and carried her across the threshold.

Gwen pushed the door closed, then turned in her husband's arms. This house wasn't home, it was wherever her husband was.

****

Thank you for reading Arthur and Gwen's story. I hope you enjoyed it. Stay tuned for more from the Proxy Bride series.

Please join my readers and me at Cyndi Raye's Readers group on Facebook.[1] (https://www.facebook.com/groups/1856224058000936/)

Keep reading for a free chapter...

---

1. https://www.facebook.com/groups/1856224058000936/

A FREE Chapter

Here's your free chapter of *An Outlaw's Honor*
This is the first story in the Brides of Mill Ridge series

"*G*ood morning, Miss Addie! What brings you to Mill Ridge so early?" Elizabeth was happy to see her mentor at the front door even if the older woman seemed to be in a state of agitation. Her dark well-kept hair was askew, along with a few strands out of place. Elizabeth noted her being a bit out of sorts for the well-managed woman everyone knew and loved.

Miss Addie took off her riding gloves as she stepped in to the foyer of the boarding house. She looked around. "You've done an excellent job here, Elizabeth. I know taking over for Sophie so quickly was difficult and I promise to send you off as a mail order bride soon, you have my word."

Elizabeth welcomed the woman with a hug. "Please, sit and have some tea."

The pot was steaming on the stove. Elizabeth was always up before her guests, planning out the days meals and making sure everything was in order for breakfast. As soon as Rose, her helper and partner for the time being, finished her early morning work, the two would start breakfast.

She poured two cups of tea, setting them on the table, along with a porcelain bowl filled with sugar and a fresh cup of cream. After serving, she sat down to wait for Miss Addie to begin. She knew it was fruitless to ask the older woman any questions until they had their tea. Her curiosity was piqued.

"How is Sophie adjusting to married life with our new sheriff, Salem Nightingale?" Miss Addie didn't seem to be in a hurry now that she was settled in at the table.

Elizabeth took a sip of tea. She had replaced Sophie, who managed the boarding house up until she married a lawman. "Wonderful, she spent the first few weeks after her honeymoon teaching me the ropes about match-making and running this place. So far I've matched a farmer with one of our wonderful ladies. Jocelyn is so happy with Fred Williams. Then there is Nanette, she's the quiet one in the crowd, she married Jonathan Myers, one of the workers at the mill. I'm very happy you are allowing me to be a matchmaker, Miss Addie, although I'll never be quite as good as you when it comes to this position."

Miss Addie shook her head. "Oh don't be prudent. You do a fine job, everyone tells me so. I'm sure you will have every chance to match up every single man in this town and beyond."

Elizabeth smiled. "If I did that, I would be out of a job."

"Nonsense, you will be married off by then to a wonderful man. When you took this position to help get the boarding house and matchmaking service started here in Mill Ridge, I promised to fulfil your original request to find you a wonderful husband, and I will."

"You are right. Miss Addie. Thank you for the kind words. I believe our Rose is sweet on one of our boarders. And, Reverend Pope feels the same way about her. She is next in line for a husband, but it may turn out I won't have to do any matchmaking after all. If you would like, please send over two more ladies for me to work with. I will begin my work with them immediately. Perhaps we will wait to see what happens between Rose and the Reverend."

"I'm impressed, Elizabeth. When we rescued all of the women from that horrible man awhile back, I had no idea so many would still be here. I was certain all of the girls would go back to their prospective homes. I'm happy to say nine of you stayed. Which is a wonderful thing since there are so many single men that need a good wife. We will build this town up just like we did Wichita Falls."

"There isn't too many women here and it can be lonely for some of us. If it weren't for Rose and Sophie, and the two ladies we just matched up, this town would be all men. We have to fix it soon, Miss Addie. Can you send me two more mail order brides? I have two extra rooms at the moment. I can place two ladies in one room and rent the other spare room out."

"Of course, if you feel ready to take on more, I'll send them over tomorrow. I think I know which two are ready to become brides. My boarding house is filled up and the five ladies left have to share rooms, making it difficult to keep tempers in check at times. Now, the reason I am truly here is to see Sheriff Nightingale.

It seems a man rode in to our town last night asking to be directed to Mill Ridge. I was hoping I beat him here since he wasn't up and about when I left this morning."

"I've been up since daylight and haven't seen or heard anyone trek through," Elizabeth answered. "Why the concern?"

"He had the looks of an outlaw. I don't want to alarm anyone but I got the impression he was on a serious quest. He was looking for someone specific. He was asking questions and showing a photo of a woman."

Elizabeth smiled. "No worries then, there are only a few women here. Sophie is happily married, tucked away in the Sheriff's cottage and Rose and I are the only two other women in town. Jocelyn and Nanette live outside of town. I wonder who he is looking for?"

"Perhaps he is here to stir up trouble and yet I don't get that awful feeling about him I usually do when someone bad passes through."

"Well, you go on and see the Sheriff. I'll need to get breakfast started. It's been a pleasure to have you here."

The moment she spoke the words, Rose came tumbling down the steps. The girl was so clumsy, she almost fell down the last three. She came in to the kitchen like a whirlwind, all smiles and tucking strands of hair in her bun. Elizabeth had sent her up to tidy the empty rooms earlier in case a guest arrived without notice, which almost always happened.

"Miss Addie! So nice to see you." Rose gave her mentor a hug, while Elizabeth looked on in amusement. The girl was simply a mess.

"Good day, ladies," Miss Addie told them before rushing out to find the sheriff.

Elizabeth turned to Rose. "Really, young lady, can you please go and straighten your hair. It looks as if you haven't combed it."

Rose giggled. "I haven't. I woke up late and pushed it back out of the way. Reverend Pope seems to think I am adorable."

"He told you that?" Elizabeth was shocked. When had the reverend been talking like that to Rose? She would need to keep a better eye on the two. After all, Elizabeth took it upon herself to mentor Rose and get her ready for her stint as a mail-order bride. If Reverend Pope wanted to marry her, he'd have to say so before Elizabeth put any time or effort into finding Rose a husband.

Rose giggled again, placing a pan on the stove. She began to crack the eggs in to the pan, one by one. "He always tells me how beautiful I am, and that I have an inspiring smile."

"He shouldn't be telling you those things in private, Rose. He needs to say if he wants to court you."

Rose sighed. "Oh, how wonderful that would be. I am afraid I'm falling for the good reverend."

"The reverend is here in the boarding house until his sanctuary is ready. The church is being re-built and the sanctuary will be done shortly. No flirting with the good man, Rose. In the meantime, Miss Addie said there is a stranger coming to town. He was in Wichita Falls last night and is looking for a woman. Steer clear of any strangers, Rose."

"I will, Elizabeth." The younger Rose turned to Elizabeth. "Please don't worry. The reverend hasn't done anything damaging. He's a man of God and his kind words were always spoken on the porch in public."

"I'm relieved to hear this, Rose. I'm afraid we may be short on eggs this morning. I see the good doctor is in town so I'm going to go over to see if I can buy some from his stock he keeps in the back yard. I shall only be about twenty minutes at the most."

"Take the empty basket and fill it up, please. We may need a few more this morning as I plan to bake a cake this afternoon."

Elizabeth took the basket, swinging the handle as she left the boarding house. Rose was going to bake a cake for the reverend after he had mentioned his love of chocolate cake. She smiled to herself. Oh, how wonderful it would be to have the growing excitement of a new love.

She didn't think she'd ever fall in love again. Perhaps Elizabeth was cursed. She had been engaged to a wonderful man. They had grown up together in the same town. Their families spent time together, they all went everywhere together.

When the outlaw gang came to their small town in Kansas, they began to torment the residents. They would rob townsfolk right off the street and no one was able to stand up to them. At first it was mild but when the gang robbed the bank and killed everyone inside, Elizabeth's whole world had changed.

Her mother, father and two younger brothers had been in the bank that day. Her fiancé brother, who owned the bank, was killed, along with his parents and grandmother.

Her fiancé had been out of town, looking over a plot of land he planned to buy. He had saved for two years to buy the land and he had promised her it would be theirs. When he had returned to find his brother and parents dead, along with the others, he had changed overnight.

His behavior had changed as he began sending telegrams to places far away. He spent less time with Elizabeth even though she needed him more than ever. Her whole family was wiped out. She had no one and yet he began to pull away from her no matter what she said or did.

His whole world revolved around waiting for each telegram, then leaving town on his horse for days at a time. His clothing began to get sloppy as if he didn't care what he looked like. Hair that was short and clipped, was now long and choppy, hiding under a wide-brimmed cowboy hat.

Elizabeth became more worried day after day. She watched his looks turn in to one like the outlaws he swore he hated.

Then one day he simply rode out of town. She had watched from her family home as he mounted his horse, knowing deep in her heart it would be the last time she'd ever see him.

The hurt that day was too immense to relive. When she had realized what he was going to do, she ran out the front door, lifting her skirts and striking up dust as she ran as fast as she could to stop him from leaving. "Wait! What are you doing?" She had cried out but he didn't look her in the eye.

"I'm a lost soul, Elizabeth. It's better this way. Go on with your life."

She stood there, willing him to look at her but he kept the brim of his hat low over his eyes. "I love you," she told him. "Doesn't that account for anything?"

A strange man she didn't recognize strolled from the saloon, dusting his hat and placing it on his head. He got on his horse and rode over to the two of them. "Ready?"

Her fiancé nodded. He directed his next words to her. "Love someone else. I'm done with this town and everyone in it."

She charged at him, reaching up to grab his leg. She tried to look up at him but he kept avoiding her eyes. "Why, my love, why? We can get through this together."

"Forget about me, Elizabeth Sheldon. I'm not your kind of man. I don't love you any more."

Shock filled her from the top of her head down to the tips of her boots. Her skirts went flying as she ran back to the haven of her family home, unable to watch the man she loved leave town. *I don't love you any more!* She'd never, ever forget those words as long as she lived.

Elizabeth stumbled as she crossed the street, realizing she was revisiting a part of her past she had shoved under the porch mat over a year ago. Was this job as match-maker causing her to relive her past? Perhaps she should tell Miss Addie to hurry and find her a husband. She closed her eyes for a moment, unsure how to move on. If she married someone else, was it fair to them knowing she'd never be able to love anyone else ever again? Her first attempt at love went horribly wrong, then the mail order bride fiasco fell through when that awful man tried to sell them as slaves. Perhaps it wasn't in the cards for her to be happy.

Realizing it was probably better this way, she decided to tell Miss Addie not to find her a husband. She would stay here, make this home. There was no reason she couldn't run the boarding house and live her life the same as Miss Addie.

"Good morning, Elizabeth. Are you here for some eggs?"

Elizabeth hadn't realized she was standing on the porch of the doctor's office. A few folks were staring. "Good morning, Nurse Ellie. May I buy some please? We're running short."

"Help yourself, Elizabeth. It's busy here today, so just put your money on the counter as you leave. I'm afraid I don't have time to have tea with you."

The good doctor and Nurse Ellie spent two days a week in Mill Ridge to help out until a doctor became available. Miss Addie donated the house and office for the doctor's use since she owned four or five different establishments in Mill Ridge, too. The doctor and his nurse-wife were trying to see all of the patients possible in the two days they had available.

So, Elizabeth was glad Nurse Ellie was too busy to talk. She didn't feel like holding a conversation with anyone today. Bringing up the past even in her mind was too distressing. She fumbled at the door to the back yard, stepping in chicken poop one too many times. After a struggle, Elizabeth collected the eggs she needed, placed the money on the counter and quickly left the doctors office without speaking to any of the patrons waiting on the porch.

"Good day, Elizabeth," Nurse Ellie told her as she came out to gather the next patient.

Elizabeth turned to wave to Nurse Ellie who was staring down the street, a look of awe all over her face. It wasn't normal for the nurse to show her emotions. She heard Ellie speaking to one of the townsfolk. "Do you know who that is?"

Elizabeth watched the exchange, wondering why the look of adoration appeared on everyone's face when they began to stare.

Slowly, some townsfolk stood. "It is him! I saw it in yesterdays paper."

"Who?" Elizabeth asked, confused.

"Why, it's all over the news. The Mill Ridge Journal put the story out yesterday. Didn't you read the paper, Elizabeth?"

"I, uh, no." She was ashamed to admit she bought the paper for her renters but was usually too busy to take time to read. Day old paper made good starter for the cook stove.

"You missed it then," Ellie noted. "I can't believe we are fortunate to have in our town the Texas Ranger who single-handedly took down the Riley Gang."

"Texas Ranger? Impressive." Even though she wasn't impressed. Where was the law when those outlaws wiped out everyone she had loved in her small Kansas town? She almost hated law men as much as she hated outlaws. Elizabeth should be ashamed of feeling so awful. The bitterness would eat her alive if she didn't keep it in check. No matter, she had to get back to help Rose with breakfast. The renters would be up and ready to be served by now.

"Have a good day, Nurse Ellie. Stop in for tea soon."

Nurse Ellie nodded, still staring at the stranger. Elizabeth shook her head, swinging around to see what the big deal was.

The horse was about two feet away. She noticed the Ranger's clothing first, as the horse was so tall she came face to face with the man's thigh. She needed him to move on so she could cross the street. When he stayed right there, she tried to keep her temper in check. "Oh for Pete sake, mister. Would you mind, I'm trying to cross the street."

Elizabeth's patience was running out. She hadn't realized she had dallied so long, it was important for her to do her job and make sure her guests were fed and on their way. She pulled the egg basket closer, gathered up her skirts with her free hand and stepped on to the street.

"Elizabeth," the raspy sound came from the man on the horse, its familiar lull causing her to raise her head in utter surprise.

Her head began to pound, the sound of his voice the only thing she understood. Voices in the background faded out. All Elizabeth saw was a pair of blue-gray eyes staring down at her.

His eyes.

The man she had loved with all her heart and soul.

She let the basket of eggs slide from her fingers. Some rolled from the basket, cracking as they hit the dirt ground.

Her heart felt as if it were pounding a mile a minute, her throat so tight she didn't have the capacity to speak. Shock overcame reality. She knew he was speaking to her, saw the motion of his mouth but had no clue how to make out the words he was saying. He began to slide from the big stallion, and yet she kept her eyes on his, like a magnet, as if she didn't dare break contact.

If she did, this would be a dream and she knew she'd wake up to realize it wasn't real.

Her throat became dry, her nostrils flared. She reached out, wanting to touch him so bad. Her body felt as if it were floating away from him instead of towards him, so she tried to grab him as he came closer. It didn't work, the clouds gathered around and pulled her away. "Noah," she whispered, his name on her lips as she fell into the darkness.

For those who want the whole thing in one shot!
Brides of Mill Ridge Box Set LIVE on Amazon[1]
(https://www.amazon.com/gp/product/B07NKCHCTB/
ref=dbs_a_def_rwt_bibl_vppi_i14)

Mail Order Brides of Wichita Falls Series

Ruby

Grace

Lily

Charity

Hannah

Rebecca

Sophie

---

1. https://www.amazon.com/gp/product/B07NKCHCTB/
ref=dbs_a_def_rwt_bibl_vppi_i14

Ellie

Jenna

Leila

Boxed Set Vol 1-8

Christmas in Wichita Falls Holiday Book

Brides of Mill Ridge Series

An Outlaws Honor

A Reverend's Rose

The Ranger's Redemption

A Doctor's Devotion

A Teacher's Treasure

A Sister's Sanctuary

Sons of Nora White Series

A Bride for Luke

A Bride for Adam

A Bride for Samuel

A Groom for Nora

A Bride for Russell

A Bride for Wesley

A Groom for Widow Young

The Pistol Ridge series

Peg Leg's Princess

Blazes' Beauty

Judge's Jewel

Creed's Confidant

Raven's Rebel

Rider's Renegade

Preacher's Pearl

Multi-Author Series Contributions

A Bride for Abel - The Proxy Brides

A Bride for Calvin - The Proxy Brides

A Tin Star for Christmas - The Belles of Wyoming

Candy Cane Christmas - Ornamental Matchmaker Book #10

An Agent for Carolina - The Pinkerton Match Maker series Book #24

A Bride for Arthur - The Proxy Brides

An Agent for Cari - The Pinkerton Match Maker series

All these books can be found by visiting
https://www.amazon.com/Cyndi-Raye/e/B00E

Don't miss out!

Visit the website below and you can sign up to receive emails whenever Cyndi Raye publishes a new book. There's no charge and no obligation.

https://books2read.com/r/B-A-PXQ-DWSDC

BOOKS 2 READ

Connecting independent readers to independent writers.